THE ADVENTURES OF ABBY AND FRIEND

THE ADVENTURES OF ABBY AND FRIEND

Connor Owens

Columbus, Ohio

This book is a work of fiction. The names, characters and events in this book are the products of the author's imagination or are used fictitiously. Any similarity to real persons living or dead is coincidental and not intended by the author.

The views and opinions expressed in this book are solely those of the author and do not reflect the views or opinions of Gatekeeper Press. Gatekeeper Press is not to be held responsible for and expressly disclaims responsibility of the content herein.

The Adventures of Abby and Friend

Published by Gatekeeper Press
2167 Stringtown Rd, Suite 109
Columbus, OH 43123-2989
www.GatekeeperPress.com

The editorial work for this book is entirely the product of the author. Gatekeeper Press did not participate in and is not responsible for any aspect of this element.

Library of Congress Control Number: 2021933026

ISBN (paperback): 9781662911132
eISBN: 9781662911149

Contents

CHAPTER ONE

The Monster in the Suit

It's a dark, crisp, and quiet autumn night in the city of Morgantown. The only sounds around are of the wind blowing and the crackling of dry, dead leaves skipping on the ground. In the distance, crickets chirp to each other deep into the night. Morgantown is known as a quiet and small place to live. It rests in the bottom of a small valley, surrounded by mountains and dense woods, with one road to enter and exit. At night, the streetlights illuminate the town, a small number of cars on the road, and most of the businesses are closed. The lights in homes and apartment buildings are off.

Everything appears to be usual until the streetlights throughout the town begin to flutter in unison. The sound of the dead leaves rustling stops abruptly, and crickets suddenly grow silent, leaving an eerie, dark silence as everything in the small town is paused in time.

Suddenly, a dog barks in the distance, the neighbor's 120-pound Mastiff, Roxy. Mrs. Leland, the owner, rushes out of her house and into the front yard, wearing her nightgown and slippers. "Roxy, come on, girl. What's gotten into you?" she whispers to the dog. She grabs onto her collar, tugging and pulling her in the house. Roxy's attention remains focused on the sky, barking and snarling, more out of fear than aggression. She fights back, attempting to free herself from her owner's grip, but Mrs. Leland finally drags the dog inside. Roxy's barks continue, now muffled inside her house.

Living next door is a fourteen-year-old girl named Abby, who is in a deep sleep, tossing and turning in her bed from a nightmare.

Abby stands alone in the middle of the woods, confused and out of breath. “Hello?” she yells out. An owl hoots, and the crickets vibrate, setting an eerie aura over Abby.

The wind blows, moving her curly hair as her voice carries in an echo, with another voice speaking to itself, “Not like this. This wasn’t a part of the—” Then it dissipates.

“Who’s out there?” Abby asks hesitantly, swallowing deeply, looking around and behind herself. Goosebumps rise on her arms and behind her neck. She startles as car tires screech somewhere in the darkness, followed by a loud crash of metal hitting something hard. She crouches to the ground with a scream and covers her ears.

Her surroundings blur as they change into a deserted street with a run-down house behind her. She stands up and notices the vines taking over the siding of the house. The tall grass covers the entrance of the home, shards of stained-glass hang from the windows, and paint peels from the shingles. Piles of rusted metal and garbage surround the perimeter of the house.

The house ignites in a fiery blaze, and the dark smoke gravitates toward Abby. She covers her face with her forearm and starts coughing, trying to get fresher air. She runs down the street until she’s out of the smoke’s reach and leans over her thighs, taking in a deep breath.

As she proceeds to walk down the road, a streetlight flickers, and she sees a flipped car in the distance. The car is severely damaged, smoke coming from the engine. Abby cautiously walks up to the vehicle. “Hello? Hello!” she yells out, ready to help as smoke fills up inside of the car, making it hard to see if anyone is inside. “Hello…” But no response as the fire spreads larger and wilder and takes over the side of the road.

Abby runs in the opposite direction, away from the wreck and into the unharmed woods beyond. The trees tower over her, their bare, weeping branches like looming shadows, and shivers take over her body, her heart fighting to beat out of her chest. She looks around in a panic and stops near a tall tree, a broken-down treehouse nestled in its branches. A blue light glows from behind the base of the tree. "Who's there?" Abby asks.

"This is not part of the plan," a voice says, supposedly coming from the orb of light.

Abby takes in a deep breath before leaping around the tree to find the source of the light. As she looks, it glows brighter, blinding her.

"Stay away!" the voice says.

A strange force envelops her, like she's standing still while the world shifts around her, and when it's gone, she stumbles. The pavement beneath her feet means her surroundings have changed again. She looks up, finding herself back on the road, but in place of the car wreck is a dead deer, blood pooled around its body. The tall pine trees on both sides of the road are on fire with heavy ash raining down like snow. The heat pricks at her skin, and the smoke fills up her lungs, suffocating her.

The voice continues, "I'm not supposed to be here…this is not good. How long have I been sleeping? Friend…he can't know about this…me…but why did he do this…what's going to happen now? So many questions unanswered," the voice says to itself, sounding panicked and confused.

Abby yells out, "Maybe we can help each other. I just need to get out of here. I can't breathe!" She struggles to catch her breath, coughing out the smoke from her lungs. Abruptly, a wave of bright blue encircles her, and the forest fire stops in time, ash hanging in midair, as if the voice heard Abby's cries for help.

"You're not supposed to be here! That was not a part of the plan!" the voice bellows back, and the force of its rage hits Abby like a wave, sending her stumbling back. Abby can feel its power and anger. The ground rumbles beneath her feet and begins to crack and fall apart into a deep, dark oblivion.

She is trapped on the last piece of road; her knees begin to buckle as she flails her arms to gain some balance. "Stop this! Please stop!" Abby begs, terrified of her uncertain destiny.

"You can't help me. You're too weak and powerless. Strengthen yourself and remember your past before it's too late. He's coming!" the voice replies anxiously.

"Who's coming? And what plan? Why do you come to me in my dreams?"

Outside of her nightmare, a loud, abrupt tapping comes from Abby's window, startling her awake. She sits up in bed, clutching her crystal, teardrop necklace, she grabs her sheets and wipes the sweat off her forehead while taking a moment to ground herself in reality. More tapping continues as she gets out of her bed to inspect. She walks toward the bay window, moving her curtains, revealing her fire escape. She sees Ping, a friendly pigeon she named secretly and calls her friend. As she opens the window, Ping flies up and perches on the fire escape banister outside.

"Ping, thank you for waking me from my bad dreams. It's been happening all week, but this time, it felt so real. They're happening more regularly. And the light spoke this time. I wonder what this all means." Ping looks at her, unfazed by her conversation as he twists his head and looks at her hands. "Oh, Ping, I don't have any food for you. I'm sorry if that's what you came for." He is not paying much attention as he puffs up and begins to clean off his loose feathers.

Abby enjoys spending time with Ping because he's always around to give her company and an ear to hear her vent out problems in her life. She named him Ping because he is always there when she needs someone to talk to—like a radar that can ping her location. Even though Ping does everything like an average pigeon would, he doesn't look like any ordinary pigeon. His feathers are worn and beaten down, dirty white with black patches on his wings, and one black circle around his eye. He walks with a limp with one leg slightly taller than the other. He's easy for Abby to find because he stands out.

Abby looks out of her second-floor bedroom window. "The voice in my dream mentioned 'He is coming.' I can't figure out what it means." Abby lies down on the bench of the bay window, failing to notice the stillness of the night, the ticking of her bedside clock silent. "Sometimes, I wish I were like you, Ping, where I can go wherever and do whatever I want without having people telling me what to do. I wouldn't be forced to be someone I'm not, and I can be alone. When times get rough, I can just fly away," she whispers as she rests her head on the window frame, daydreaming places she would fly to. Ping looks up with his head tilted to the side, like he's listening for something, getting Abby's attention. "What's wrong?"

Thunder rumbles in the distance, but there's not a single cloud in the sky. Ping darts his head around, startled by the sound, then flies away. A second rumble follows soon after the first but, this time, with a blue flicker of light behind the hills, catching Abby by surprise as she watches out the window. The wind abruptly begins to gust, whipping the curtains in her bedroom in all directions.

Roxy barks up at the sky, becoming more aggressive and frantic, saliva spraying across the windowpane. Abby takes a second glance out her window and is shocked to see the town at a standstill. The trees are bent from the wind, dead leaves free-floating on the streets and sidewalk. Roxy continues to bark until it turns into a desperate yelp, then silence. The atmosphere changes, muted and unnerving, and Abby suspects she is the only witness over the town. It's so quiet her own breathing is suddenly deafening. She holds her breath, anxious to listen to the silence, but her heartbeat in her ears drowns it out.

A loud bang is heard from behind the mountains that engulfs the town. Its powerful rumbles vibrate with the streetlights flickering out of control. A second bang goes off in the distance. In the streets of Morgantown, sparks fly into the air—from where, Abby doesn't know—and onto Isabella Avenue, a couple blocks over from her perch on Main Street.

She shudders with fear as a large, bright blue shockwave glows and branches out of the sky, barreling down the hilltops toward the town. She tries to keep her eyes open, but the light is too blinding. The warmth of the light washes over her as it gets closer. The air suddenly grows still, and the heat of the glow goes away, leaving an unsettled stillness throughout the town. The leaves and the curtains on Abby's window stop in motion. Abby fears her nightmares are becoming a reality, and she contemplates a plan to get away as she tries to navigate through her room.

Her necklace lifts from her chest, pointing up at the bright light. Abby stands motionless, unsure how to handle an inanimate object coming to life around her neck. She is both confused and curious at what she's witnessing, at a loss for words. "Cece!" Abby cries out for her foster parent, asleep in the next room, but with no response. The crystal glows sapphire, shining as it follows the comet. The chain digs into the back of her neck.

The expansion of light fans over the small city, as it makes its way to Abby's window. Abby has no time to take cover. The supernatural blast propels her away from the window and down to the floor. She scrambles onto her feet, running to her door and turning the handle, but it is forced shut. She turns back to the window and approaching comet, a scream frozen in her throat. Her necklace struggles to meet it as its light becomes blinding, and Abby falls to the floor, feeling her way around her room, trying to hide.

Abby covers her eyes as she feels a presence close by. Groaning and fast ticking sounds come from the corner of her room. Abby is terrified and still unable to see, but she hears footsteps walking toward her. With every step, the groaning and ticking noises become louder, along with deep, heavy breathing. A long exhale blows on to Abby, pushing her hair to the side, making her too afraid to move.

Abby slowly opens her eyes, adjusting her vision. A silhouette of a frail and towering monster hovers over her. Abby screams, "Get away from me!" She tries to crawl away toward her bed, glancing at her wall where the silhouette reaches for her, and she cries out in terror once again but even louder, hoping someone, anyone, will hear her. "Cece, help, help!" But nothing. Abby gets half of her body under her bed before a cold hand grabs her ankle, dragging her out. The bright light from outside the window slowly dims, revealing the true monster behind the profile.

The monster's very tall and skinny with extended hands, arms, and legs. It wears a men's suit with a long, skinny tie; blazer; dress pants; and shoes, all too short with its wrists and ankles exposed. Abby screams when she looks higher to its face; the monster has no eyes but deep, empty sockets atop high cheekbones. It also lacks a nose or ears, just small openings where they are supposed to be. The monster's mouth extends outward with large, exposed teeth.

It stumbles, leaning against Abby's tall dresser as it tries to hold its body up, letting out a heavy sigh and growl. It looks at itself in the dresser mirror, shaking its head in disgust, in a lot of pain. With one hand on the dresser, it presses the other inside its blazer, holding its side. It is badly wounded with blood covering its hand.

As Abby takes a deep breath, the monster quickly lifts its hand up toward her. The palm of its hand glows, resulting in Abby's inability to move and speak. Its power courses through her, leaving her feeling defenseless and worried about its intentions.

It holds out a necklace laced in between its fingers. Abby scrutinizes the gem, and her stomach drops; the necklace is identical to the one around her neck. The only difference, underneath the blood and dirt, is a crack across the crystal.

It collapses on the floor, landing on its knees in front of her. Abby, still unable to move her body, can feel the cold exhale from the monster's nostrils as it whimpers and groans in pain. She notices her necklace still pointing at the monster but it's no longer glowing. She is terrified—fire and smoke are visible outside her window, like her dream—but doesn't feel threatened at this point. It breathes heavily over her, reaching out, touching her curly hair, and sighing. It exposes the hand that was under its blazer, filled with blood, dark blue with a tar-like consistency. While opening its mouth, a blue glow comes out. She is in shock, trying to convince herself this is a dream, but it's all too much. She faints.

A knock is heard from Abby's bedroom door, getting louder and louder. Startled, Abby finally awakens, sitting up in bed. She darts her eyes around—nothing unusual or out of place— and she releases a sigh of relief when she realizes it's morning. "It was all just a bad dream," she says to herself.

"Girl, girl! You better not be late for school," Cece says on the other side of the door.

"I'm up, Cece, I'm getting ready," Abby responds.

"You're late," she firmly snaps back. Abby hears her walk farther down the hall. Cece is known to be very confrontational and blunt. She expresses what's on her mind, unaware of how her words may offend someone else. Cece is an older woman who's a stickler for following the rules, and she always makes sure Abby obeys them.

Abby has been living with Cece on and off, but most of the time, she lives with her. She would have to leave sometimes because she was a perennial candidate for being adopted many times, but for Abby, it never felt right. To her, it felt forced, littering her with gifts, saying she was home now. Some couples would bring the whole family of strangers over, making it impossible for Abby not to be the center of attention, exactly where she didn't want to be.

Abby checks the time; school will be starting soon. She runs straight to her window, opening her blinds so the sun beams through. She looks out and watches kids heading to school with their oversized backpacks, hopping on the school buses. Businesses open for the day, and cars commute to work. The streets are littered with leaves, branches, and pieces of roofing, but nobody seems fazed by their surroundings. As she looks around, she thinks, *Maybe it was just a bad storm?*

She suddenly hears a voice say, "Time can't stop." Her head whips around, searching for the source, but her room is empty. Abby's attention reverts to the time. Twenty minutes, the clock reads, for her to get to school on time. In a frantic rush, she puts her t-shirt, jeans, and gray, hooded sweatshirt on as she gets ready for school.

As Abby rushes out of her bedroom, her shoe steps in something thick and moist. She glances down at a stain in the carpet. A dark, sticky, tar-like substance. Her breathing hitches as her eyes follow the trail running from her dresser, the same spot where the monster had bled, to the top of her dresser, discovering an old jam sandwich that had fallen over. With a sigh of relief, she runs out of her room and down the stairs, leaving the brownstone.

She runs to school with her backpack weighing her down, stepping over large branches and other debris from the overnight storm. She makes it down Main Street, where the stores act as a halfway point to Abby's school, and already, she is losing stamina and speed, trying to catch her breath.

Her legs begin to cramp, but she tries to push on. She misses a step, causing her to stumble over herself with her heavy backpack swinging, making her more unstable. Abby feels a push on her back, causing her to trip forward into a puddle on the sidewalk, making a large splash. Her clothes are soaked and stained in muddy water as she lies in the puddle, too embarrassed and out of breath to get up.

When she finds the strength to pull herself up, a voice exclaims beside her, "My suit, my favorite suit," followed by a deep sigh of frustration. "Girl, look what you did to my suit!" a disgruntled man's voice says.

Abby looks up at the tall figure and gasps at his startling resemblance to the monster. His diamond-shaped face is timeworn with wrinkles around his forehead, nose, and mouth. His small, brown eyes, accented with heavy, dark bags, glares down a wide-bridged nose at her, but she's more focused on the large ears protruding from the sides of his head.

Abby recognizes his face. Hudson Carter, a well-known salesman. "The one you call for a new home or if you need a helping hand." That's what his ads say all over the town's stores, television commercials, and even property lawn billboards. Wherever you look in town, he's there. People find him to be rude, selfish, and a cheap conman with no real work, but he still finds a way to look busy trying to find work and scam people in the process.

She glances behind her, finds no one there, no culprit to the crime of pushing her, then turns back to Mr. Carter. His suit is speckled with water and mud, and he points at the cleaners behind him. "I just came out of there with my new fitted suit, and it's not cheap. I have somewhere especially important to go today, and you, *you*—" Mr. Carter locks eyes with Abby, and his demeanor changes from angry to astounded.

A voice talks to her in her mind. "Go!" The concern in its voice is lost on her as a heavy, deep groaning coming from the alley next to the cleaners distracts her, sounding just like the monster in her dream.

She tries to walk past Mr. Carter, wanting to listen to the voice, as she feels endangered. "I'm sorry, sir, but I have to go to school," she says in a low and soft voice, not trying to provoke any more trouble.

"Wait right there!" He reaches down to grab her wrist, but she is too quick, moving out of the way just in time and racing down the block to make it to school on time. "You won't be getting away from this that easily!" he calls out before losing sight of her.

Abby finally arrives at school. It's 8:43 a.m., and she is late for the first time. She makes her way up to the school's main entrance and takes a deep breath as she pushes open the doors of Morgantown High to the unexpected. The hallway bustles with activity, students chatting in their groups, lockers hanging open, and most students waiting for class to start. By this time, the halls should be quiet and empty. Abby looks at the nearest clock on the wall, reading 7:43 a.m. "Impossible," she mumbles to herself, trying to understand how she was late a second ago but now isn't.

"Time can be tricky," the voice says.

"Who are you, and why am I the only one who can hear you?" Abby replies, some students staring at her like she's crazy. Abby ducks her head to avoid standing out as she continues to walk down the hallway to her red locker, number fifteen. She opens it to get her math book when she realizes she's being watched, laughter and mumbling behind her.

"Now I guess she's homeless. Sleeping in some back-alley dumpster and dragging her filth here," one girl says while giggling. Abby looks down at her shirt and sees the now-dried mud stains from tripping in the puddle. Abby sighs to herself, embarrassed, and she doesn't want to turn around. More students are staring at her and chiming in with their own insults and taunts.

"Look how dirty she is."

"Hey, guys, do you smell that?"

"That's gross!"

"Do you even shower?" The first bell rings, interrupting the laughter. Abby turns away from her locker as she closes it and tries to use her textbook to cover the stains. As she begins to walk away, a sudden nudge to her back makes her stumble and drop her book to catch herself, bumping into a student bystander. "Sorry, sorry, sorry," she says, out of sorts, trying to get out of the hallway as she looks up and sees Jennifer and Rachel, better known as The Twins. They're bullies, especially Jennifer, the leader and master manipulator, and they happen to share most of their classes with Abby.

She should have known it was them. Jennifer is the most popular girl in their high school and captain of the cheerleading squad. She's more of the problem for Abby than her autistic twin sister, Rachel. She is the nicer of the two but tends to get caught up in Jennifer's battles as the bystander. Abby suffers everyday with Jennifer's bullying; she feels like she only does it to try to become more popular. It's always been difficult for Abby to stand up for herself.

"Get your dirty hands off me, Foster Trash!" Jennifer says with a smirk, wanting a fight while pushing Abby off her.

Rachel walks over, lightly tugs on Abby's hair. "I always liked your hair," she says, distracted, her big eyes magnified by her glasses.

"Well?!" Jennifer snaps at Rachel.

"What? Oh, yeah." Rachel puts her backpack on the floor, opening it up. It's overly stuffed with wrinkled papers, bitten pencils, and old candy. Some teenagers laugh at Rachel as they pass on their way to class. Their laughter flusters her as she searches her bag. A letter falls out with Rachel unaware.

Jennifer begins to lose her temper. "It's right there…no, there… the other side!"

Rachel finds the letter on the ground as she tries to keep her large glasses on her face; she apologizes to Jennifer before handing the letter to Abby. "This is for you, Abby. I really hope you like it. I'm the one who did the drawing," she says with a smile on her face, still admiring Abby's curly hair. Some students linger in the hallway, struggling to hold in their laughs toward Rachel as Jennifer gives them evil stares. Abby takes the letter but refuses to open it.

"You're going to read it, go ahead. Read it out loud. We are all waiting!" Jennifer says with her arms crossed. Abby's face burns with humiliation, looking down at the letter. Jennifer loses her patience as some begin to murmur under their breath, one saying aloud, "Wow, is Abby really standing up to Jennifer?" Jennifer shoves Abby, pinning her up against her locker.

"I don't want any trouble," Abby says, pleading with one of Jennifer's friends.

"Fight!"

"Read the letter out loud or get punched in the face. You have until the count of three. One, two…" Jennifer raises her hand into a fist.

"What are you doing? Fight her already," the voice in Abby's mind says.

She closes her eyes and clenches her fist. Her necklace quivers against her chest and lights up through her shirt. Abby quickly reaches up to hold onto the crystal. The students chanting, "Fight, fight, fight…" echoes away into silence. She opens her eyes, but her school is almost unrecognizable.

She stands alone in the hallway in a daze, her necklace the only light illuminating the ash falling to the floor. The air is warm and smells burnt. Abby looks around; her body begins to sweat and tense up. "Hello!" Her voice echoes back to her. As she walks farther down the hall, her shoes scuff over cracked paint debris on the floors. The ceiling peppers ash onto her hair. "Is anyone there?" she hesitantly asks. Abby turns around, and her necklace points ahead of her. She follows it left of the main entrance. Outside the doors, it looks like a natural disaster or war took place.

Most of Morgantown is demolished with no trace of life. The trees are burnt to splintering, black charcoal. Bodies crowd the street, some upright and some in a running position, all burnt to cinders, and the desperation of their last moments leaves a mark on her heart. As far as she can see, Court Square, the courtyard in front of the courthouse, is the only spot unaffected, as it is protected by a blue dome, something supernatural she has never seen before.

The high school doors burst open with a warm gust of wind, blowing down the hallway, quickly turning cold. Abby hears the groaning and clicking sounds from her dream. As Abby's necklace glows brighter, she begins to walk backwards. The grunting sounds coming from the monster become louder.

"Stay away from me, stay away!" she yells, echoing through the empty hallways. The monster appears, limping up the stairs of the school's entrance, still wounded and holding its side. Her necklace vibrates as it walks toward her. It points at her, lowering his hand to her necklace. "Stay away from me!" It continues slowly while limping and trying to hold itself up. The closer it gets to Abby, the greater her realization that this is happening, this is real.

She tries to run away, but it quickly opens its hand, and a pulse of glowing, blue energy sprouts out and down the hallway. Abby is stuck and unable to move again. It plods closer, leaning so close they are now face-to-face. As its empty sockets bore into her, she wonders who will mourn her if this monster kills her. Will Ping? Will Cece? Tears stream down her cheeks, and she prays this isn't how she ends.

The monster sighs an exhale of frustration. The breath brushes over her hair, sending ash flying everywhere. Abby can see its leather-like skin, revealing the scars all over its body, the sheer number of them leading her mind to torture. The monster reaches over and pauses to feel Abby's face with a boney, cold hand, making a whimpering noise. In that moment, she feels as if it is trying to comfort her. Immediately, its mood shifts, the pain and frustration giving way to hope. For reasons she can't explain, she embraces its touch and, with it, a sense of familiarity, as though she understands and knows who it is, but she can't quite figure out how and why. It's too confusing, and Abby just wants to go back to living her usual life, even if that means being bullied by Jennifer and Rachel. She wants the devastation that happened to Morgantown to dissipate.

The monster's hand begins to glow while it puts its thumb on her forehead. There is a radiant light with its power, leaving a tingling impression on her skin. The glow of its hand reminds her of the invisible bonds rooting her in place. What is it doing now? Stealing her memories? Altering them? The familiarity from a moment ago is washed away by a new wave of fear, and Abby gathers her strength, takes a deep breath, eyes closed, and lets out, "Leave me alone!"

The warmth dissipates, and laughter erupts around her, deafening after the silence, from the students in the hallway. Abby is still face-to-face with Jennifer, whose mouth hangs open, appalled Abby is standing up for herself. Abby realizes what was intended for the monster had actually been yelled at Jennifer. Someone in the crowd says toward Jennifer, "You're not going to take that, are you?" She clenches her teeth together.

Abby tries to apologize, "I'm…sorry, Jennifer. I…I didn't… I promise that wasn't toward you."

"Oh, Abby, you don't know what you just got yourself into." Jennifer grins. She cracks her knuckles and grabs Abby by her hair, dragging her to the girl's bathroom. Abby struggles against her grip, backing away from the restroom doors.

Students laugh and start chanting again, "Fight, fight, fight!" Abby tries to hold on to the sides of the door frame, but Jennifer's cheerleading crew push her hands away, allowing Jennifer to yank Abby's hair and drag her into the bathroom stall.

"Come on, Abby, it's time to wash up." With an evil smirk, Jennifer forces Abby's head into the toilet. Abby tries to catch her breath, begging Jennifer to stop, but with every plea, Abby's face gets dunked again as the laughter gets louder. "Look at this, girls; even when you clean her, she still looks like foster trash," Jennifer says while letting go of Abby's hair.

The sound of teachers roaming the halls and ushering children into classrooms grows louder, prompting Jennifer and her group to leave the bathroom. "Oh, this is so going viral!" one of the girls says as she finishes recording.

As they all leave the restroom, Abby sits up from the toilet, her head and clothes soaking wet. She curls up on the floor, tired and defeated, and with her last bit of strength fueled with rage, she yells out, "Why me? Why does this always happen to me?!" Her hand slams against the cold tile floor. She starts to cry while sitting on the floor with her arms wrapped around her legs, pulling them close to her chest. Her life can't get any harder. What makes it worse is knowing there is no one she trusts or feels comfortable with to help guide her through times like this.

"I used to ask myself the same question," the voice in her head replies.

"Who are you, and why are you in my head?"

"First, I am not in your head; I'm just in you. Secondly, my story is much longer than yours, and it's going to take too much time to explain, which we don't have."

Abby takes a second to think. "This monster that's following me. Am I in danger?"

"No and yes, but not by what you think you are. It's all too puzzling to say in one breath, but we don't have much time. If I speak too long, he will know."

"You mean the monster? Do you know who he is?" Abby says.

"Only if you remembered the past," the voice replies.

The second bell rings. "Wait, don't go. What does he want from me? Hello…?" But no answer.

Abby gets up from the cold tiled floor and attempts to dry off her hair with a paper towel. She looks up at her reflection, but when she sees how wet and dirty she is, her sadness quickly turns into rage. She doesn't feel deserving of this treatment. "This is all because of him, but I just don't know what you want from me," Abby says while looking down at her necklace. It begins to glow a bit, and her hair and clothes start drying rapidly.

"Learn the craft of time," the voice says with her necklace glowing. Her clothes are dried and clean from the power from her necklace. This leaves Abby speechless and puts a smirk on her face as she heads to her first period.

As midday approaches, students roam the halls toward the cafeteria where a line has already formed. Abby joins the line and glances at the already overcrowded room, spotting an empty table near the doors.

A student leaving the line bumps into Abby's shoulder while heading toward a nearby table. "Watch where you're going!"

All too used to the abuse, Abby keeps moving ahead. Today's menu includes mashed potatoes and gravy, steak, and green beans, none of which looks as good as it sounds.

The lunch lady scoops the food and carelessly slaps it onto her tray. Her disposable apron and vinyl gloves already covered in stains, the older lady pushes up her glasses, calling, "Next!"

Abby picks up a disposable plastic utensil set and a small carton of chocolate milk. As she walks to her table, she can't help but notice other students staring at her and looking at their phones. She finally sits down, alone, putting her hood over her head, trying to hide herself. Not hungry, she begins to play with her soggy mashed potatoes and green beans, and her mind keeps wandering back to the monster and that voice.

Laugher erupts from the table in front of her where the jocks and cheerleaders sit, and it pulls her from her thoughts. They, too, are glancing and pointing at her. Her face burns with embarrassment as she realizes they are watching the video of her getting bog-washed, gaining her more attention than she is used to. Abby quickly gets up and dumps her tray in the nearby trash, uncomfortable with the unwanted attention, and she leaves the lunchroom.

Walking down the hallway, someone calls for her. Abby stops and turns around. It's Ms. Perez, her guidance counselor. "Hey, is everything okay?" Ms. Perez asks.

"Yeah, everything is fine," Abby says, looking down, unable to fake her emotions.

"Are you sure? You seem a bit down." Ms. Perez tilts her head worriedly, trying to look at Abby's face.

"Yeah, I'm fine. I just wanted to go out for some air before lunch is over," Abby says, taking a few steps back.

"Well, before you leave, I wanted to hand you this flyer. I want you to consider attending the school's fall gathering. There will be games and lots of food. Trust me, it will be fun. I think it will help you see the good in some of the kids in the school. I know it can be hard, but I would like for you to give it a shot. What do you say? Will you think about it?"

Abby snatches the flyer and stuffs it in her sweater pocket. "I'll think about it."

"Okay, well, can you meet me tomorrow? Say fifth period? We have some things to discuss."

"Sure thing," Abby says, finally turning away from Ms. Perez and heading toward the exit.

"Well, have a good rest of your day."

Abby ventures outside to get some much-needed fresh air and to avoid the attention. She walks past the playground swings and monkey bars, past the baseball diamond, and into the open field where there is an old dogwood tree, thankfully ignored by everyone and the perfect spot for Abby to reflect. She runs her hand across the bark of the tree.

Her necklace glows with the voice coming back to Abby, "So you just let them step on you like that? Stand up for yourself!"

"It's much harder than it looks."

"No, you just make it hard for yourself, making it easy for them to prey on you because they see you as weak. I'll help you."

"Then what should I see you as?"

"See me as your other half."

"My other half? Why should I trust you?"

"Because if it wasn't for me, you would still be dirty and wet, and I don't even get a thank you."

"What about the monster? Why does he come to me, and why is he hurt?"

"Well, let's not call him a monster. He is an ally, and he can be more than that. Sometimes, he has a hard time showing it, but he means well. I can't tell you everything, and I have questions too, but I have to be a secret to him. It can mess with time. But right now, he needs you more than you need him."

Lunch ends, and the rest of the school day moves on. Abby enters her final class of the day, all eyes are on her while she makes her way to her desk by the window. Mr. Booker, her English teacher, walks around the class, handing out everyone's test grades, and when he makes it to Abby, he places the test results on her desk. Abby scored an A+. This is the only good news she's received all day. It's been hard for her to concentrate in her classes because she can't stop thinking about what the voice said about the monster.

Abby tries to remember the monster's distinct face by drawing it on the side of her class worksheet. The sockets without eyes, his protruding jaw, and long hands in the suit that doesn't fit his towering height. She rests her pencil on the side of her desk and watches it slowly tilt toward the window. A tall silhouette stands down in the open field on the border of the football yard and dense woods. The silhouette takes one step forward, and she sees the monster. Abby squints at him, trying to see the gesture he makes at her. He points at his head.

Something hits the back of her own. When she turns around, she sees it was Jennifer. "She's so slow!" a boy from the class says. Abby's gaze drops to her slightly opened backpack, the letter Rachel gave her sitting on top. She looks back out the window and doesn't see the monster anymore. The final bell rings with all the students chattering in their groups as they gather their belongings. Mr. Booker claps his hands, getting all the students' attention.

"Listen up! Before all of you leave, please take one of the flyers for the up-and-coming fall gathering social this week. There will be games to play, prizes to win, movies to watch, and plenty of food to eat. So do not be off that day. If you want to participate in the games, the sign-up sheet is out in the hall."

Some kids roll their eyes and others seem excited for the games to play. Abby waits for everybody to leave so she is not targeted again.

The class empties out, leaving Abby and Mr. Booker behind. He starts to gather his belongings and sees Abby still in the classroom. "What are you still doing here? You should be on your way home." Sounding concerned, he approaches Abby and leans on a nearby desk. "Let me guess, you're waiting for certain people to leave?"

She nods, too embarrassed to explain why.

"I see. Abby, did you ever play baseball? Well, imagine baseball as life. Sometimes, the pitcher will throw some fast or curve balls and maybe a crazy knuckle ball, but that's life. Every day, you don't know what opportunity life is going to throw at you, but you as the batter must choose. What do you want in life? Choose your ball carefully because once you swing, there's no going back, and it's up to you to decide how you want to hit it."

Abby thinks about the monster and being persistent on finding out what it wants, briefly blocking out what Mr. Booker is saying.

"Maybe they will leave you alone," he says.

"Mr. Booker, what if I have a bigger problem than just my classmates?"

"Like what?" he asks.

"I don't know, maybe a powerful creature from another planet seeking help in order to prevent the apocalypse." Abby's expression quickly morphs from deadpan to humorous.

Mr. Booker pauses for a moment and starts to chuckle. "Whatever it is, it's up to you to make things that surround your life right. Be more persistent. Get to the bottom of your problems and address them. Now I must get going. I'll leave you and let you gather your things; no rush." He gets up and puts the marked papers into his briefcase.

"Thanks for the advice," Abby says. Mr. Booker walks out of the classroom.

Abby reaches into her bag to read the letter. Unfolding it, it reads:

Dear Foster Trash,
Do all of us in the school a favor and never come back. No one likes you, and no one ever will. That is why you have no parents and no friends.

On the bottom of the letter is a poorly drawn image of two stick figures with the words "Mother" and "Father" written on top. There is an X crossing them out in red marker. Tears run down her face. She can only wish she knew who her parents were.

Abby's necklace glows faintly. "Stop it and just leave me alone!" Crushing the letter in her hand, she stands up from her seat and glares out the window one more time. Abby sees the monster once more, this time his stance more aggressive. He leans up against an old, rotting tree. His protruding, heavy brow casts a dark shadow in his deep eye sockets, making him look menacing, but it doesn't deter Abby. She picks up her backpack angrily. "I have had enough," Abby mumbles to herself. She walks out of the classroom into the hallway, ready to meet with the monster once and for all.

CHAPTER TWO

Power Through the Light

Abby walks to the back exit leading to the schoolyard, swinging the door open with rage. She marches her way down the stairs and toward the field where she notices Ping standing on top of the fence. He flaps his wings forcefully, trying to get Abby's attention. "Not now, Ping," she lashes out and marches onto the dry, grassy field, passing the old dogwood tree where the jocks are starting to warm up for practice. Meanwhile, Abby's eyes fixate on the edge of the woods.

"Are you sure you are ready for this?" the voice says.

"I have no other choice. I want to know what he wants, and that goes for you too. I don't know what you both want from me."

"It has nothing to do with what I want from you. I'm in the same boat as you are. I have been asleep for a long time and was awoken when he came."

"Yeah, well then, who is he? It seems like you both know each other," Abby says.

"It is a complicated story, but he was my good friend, and we did a lot together."

"You never seem to let me know why I'm being targeted. If you both were such good friends, why does he want me and not you?" Abby asks. She makes her way to the edge where the dense woods begin, taking in a heavy breath before entering, placing one foot into the tall and overgrown shrubbery.

"Abby, it's too much to explain. All of this was not a part of the plan."

Abby stumbles. "Did you just say 'a part of the plan'? So you were in my dream? You're the blue light!"

"I am not what I once was. I was different. You must promise me you won't tell him I'm alive. His attempt to save me didn't work."

"Save you? What happened?"

"Hey, where do you think you're going?" a voice yells out in the distance, grabbing her attention. Abby turns around to one of the senior football players in his practice uniform. As he's waving his arms, he jogs toward her. "You know you're not allowed to go into the woods," he says, concerned. Abby looks at him, confused. "Didn't you ever hear the story about the girl who went into the woods playing hooky? She walked in and never came out."

The voice says, "I remember that story because that was me a long time ago. We were on a mission. Friend and I were facing a creature, who swallowed something very important to us."

Abby gasps in shock. "So you lived here in Morgantown also? How old are you?" she asks, forgetting the senior player standing right in front of her.

The senior responds to her question. "Yeah, I'm seventeen..." He continues to ramble on with the voice interrupting inside her head, "If you want to know what he wants, you should go now. He came back for a reason. I need to know why he has returned."

Abby agrees, interrupting the senior, "I'm so sorry, but I think I'll take my chances." Before he can speak another word of concern, she turns to the woods and continues to walk. Within a couple of feet, the light dims, as the woods conceal any sunlight. Some time passes as she treks deeper with no sight or sign of the monster. All she can hear are the swaying of the tall oak and pine trees and the crunching of dead leaves and branches beneath her feet. A massive rock appears on her trail. She climbs on top, the wet moss soaking through her jeans, to search for any signs or clues. "I know you're out there!" she yells.

Her necklace lifts, glowing bright blue, pointing to her left—a sign she was desperately looking for. She jumps off the rock and begins to run out in the direction of the necklace. She runs to her left and sharply right, ducking beneath the branches. The necklace brings her on a wild chase, taking her farther and farther into the woods, her school and Morgantown far out of sight.

The temperature plummets, sending a shiver of anxiety down her spine. Abby starts to lose hope and patience. Consumed by the woods, her agitation grows while aimlessly following her necklace, still illuminating brightly, pointing straight ahead. Her surroundings feel familiar. She remembers being here but only in her dreams. Abby looks down at her glowing necklace, letting out a long sigh. "There is something you want from me, but even when I come to you, you still find a way to make it difficult," Abby says aloud, knowing he is listening. "I know you're here." The necklace moves, and she continues.

More time passes as she follows her necklace in what feels like circles and is proven moments later when she bumps into the same large, mossy rock in the center of the woods. Abby's necklace begins to spin around her neck, glowing brighter. She feels a warm, burning sensation on her neck. Abby is finally fed up with what feels like a childish game. She yells out, "Show yourself!" She picks up a dead branch by her foot, leaning up against the rock and blindly swinging it in front of her.

Her swing ends up more powerful than she anticipated, and she loses her grip on the branch, hearing it fly into the darkness. The only sound is of the branch whipping through the air and hitting a tree, landing on dead leaves. Abby collapses to her knees, exhausted from running; she puts her hands over her face and begins to weep. The woods are quiet and eerie. Past her curfew,

Abby worries about how she's going to find her way home. Cece has only two rules: first, to do well in school, and second, to be home before dark. "I am sick and tired of playing these stupid games! I don't know what you want from me, but I'm done!"

As Abby gets up and ponders how to navigate out of the woods, she feels tugging on her necklace. Unusual noises echo in the distance, leaves crunching followed by dragging, like long, clumsy steps, and they approach fast, terrifying her. "Show yourself...I know that's you. Show yourself, monster!" she yells louder.

The necklace rattles and glows brighter, moving from left to right around Abby's neck. A twig snaps above her, high in the trees. Her head whips up, expecting to find the monster lurking in the branches, but it's Ping, staring down at her with beady eyes. He swoops down off the tree branch and flies over Abby and in the direction the necklace is pointing. "Ping, no, don't go over there!" She waves her hands franticly, hoping Ping will stop or turn away.

A large hand emerges from behind a thick tree trunk, grabbing Ping with lengthy fingers. An explosion of feathers flies out of the monster's grip and fall slowly to the ground. There is a brief silence except for Ping's bones breaking under pressure. Abby comes to the quick, horrifying realization Ping was just killed by the monster.

"No, no, no, Ping!" She runs forward. "Let go of him, you monster!" The monster grips Ping tighter, growling before he lets go of what is left of him, a fine grain of dust and feathers. Abby stares open-mouthed at the remains of her only friend.

He sighs, followed by a roar and some clicks. He slowly walks forward, revealing himself, and leans up against a big oak tree, hunching over, breathing heavily. There is a short pause before Abby begins asking questions. "Who are you, and what are you?"

The monster pushes his body up, supporting himself against some tree branches. He moves toward Abby, and as he gets closer, her necklace moves up her neck, pointing at him. The monster's palm begins to glow as he holds his wound, and she notices it slowly starting to heal. Abby can't believe what she's witnessing.

"You might think this is barbaric, but it is how he survives. He feeds to gain his powers back, but this isn't enough. He won't hurt you; he wants to protect you," the voice explains. The light coming from the monster's hand starts to fade. He clenches his hand in pain.

"How did you get hurt?" Abby says to the monster as her anger moves to the back burner to make room for her growing concern for the monster. He takes a couple of short steps before collapsing to the ground, unable to move. "I don't know what to do to help you." He breathes heavily in pain. She does not feel threatened but instead the need to help.

He looks at her, letting out a big sigh. He stretches out his long arms, pointing at his wound, as if answering the question "This is me."

"You can understand me?"

The monster gives Abby a nod.

Her eyes grow large. "So you can understand me. Why do you keep on following me?"

He shakes his head as he raises one of his arms and points at his wrist.

"No time? What are you running from?"

He replies with a nod, pointing at Abby, then to his head, puzzling her. Abby has another question ready on her tongue, but she is quickly interrupted by the monster, tapping harder on his wrist.

He clenches his wound in pain, the other hand fisted on the ground. Blood drips like a slow, leaky faucet onto the dirt by his fist. The voice said he was healing but not fast enough. The necklace dims in and out, following the same rhythm of the monster's heavy breathing, confirming Abby's suspicion that this necklace is a part of him and his powers.

"Is this necklace yours?"

The monster nods yes with a lingering, awkward silence.

"So why do I have your necklace?"

He lowers his hand and points at the ground, showing her where to stand. She takes one step forward, and he snatches Abby's arm in a tight grip. Abby begins to panic, trying to pull away while he fights to hold onto her. The monster squeezes her arm forcefully, dragging her to her knees. The necklace illuminates so radiantly Abby is astounded as she watches her hands glow just like his.

"Harness that power; learn to control it," the voice says.

The warm, supernatural tingling runs up her arm and makes her panic even more. "Get off of me!"

She gapes at the sudden deepening of her voice. Her eyes roll into the back of her head as she growls demonically. Power flows through her veins, and Abby's eyes turn a bright, glowing blue.

The monster flinches away from her power. While losing his grip, leaves, branches, and the large, mossy boulder lift in the forest around Abby, and he attempts to shake her out of this state. Her eyes slowly fade back to normal, but her hand is still glowing. When she gains consciousness, she kicks and punches to get away from the monster, but he grabs Abby's glowing hand and places it on his wound. His blood is warm and wet against her fingers, his skin frighteningly cold. The wound closes at her touch, and his skin tightens. Abby turns her face away and shuts her eyes. The monster lifts her hand away from his wound.

When she opens her eyes, she feels the warm sun hitting her cold body. Abby looks around and quickly realizes she is no longer in the dense woods. Instead, she is back in the open field on the edge of the school's property where she last encountered the senior. Abby, breathing a sigh of relief, hopes she can finally go home. She glances down at her hands, and they appear normal. She stares around and cannot help but feel like a target. Abby sees the football players warming up and birds flying in the air. As she approaches, she realizes everyone is immobile. The birds are frozen in flight, and the players are still holding equipment.

Abby hears footsteps coming from behind her in the woods. She turns around, and the monster is standing behind a narrow tree, quiet and still. A long pause grows between them. "If this necklace is that important to you, then you can have it," Abby says. As she attempts to remove her necklace, the monster extends his hand out toward her. "No, I don't want to go with you. You killed my friend!" Abby begins to shed tears of anger. "How can I trust you?" Abby takes a couple of steps back.

He extends his hand farther and snaps his fingers. To Abby's surprise, Ping appears fully intact, swooping down past her, and rests on the monster's long finger. Ping looks at Abby before flying away, lifting off, then turning to dust. Suddenly, the birds in the distance begin to fly in reverse; the athletes on the field walk backward in the direction of the school; other students leaving campus start walking back into the school.

The trees begin to bend and sway forcefully. However, Abby can't hear any sound of the rewinding movements. "Are you doing this?" Distracted by the students, she focuses on him, now standing across from her with his hand glowing blue. "Please stop!" He snaps his fingers once more, listening to her command and stopping time. "What's your name, and what do you want from me?"

The sound of weeping comes from behind a tree, and she spins around, searching for the source. Abby considers running away, but the monster turns toward her. Allowing him to get closer, the monster makes some clicking noises and lends out his hand. Abby tenses up. She closes her eyes for a brief moment, and when she opens them, the monster is holding the letter Jennifer and Rachel gave her.

"Hey, where did you get that? Give it back!" She reaches for it, but he holds it just out of her reach. He opens the letter and points to the word "Friend." As Abby tries to figure out what he's hinting to her, he points at "Friend" once more. "Is your name Friend?"

"Yes, yes! Do you remember who he is?" the voice says, confirming his name to Abby.

"No, how could I remember?" The monster, Friend, with no warning, pushes Abby back. She loses her footing on the grassy field and falls onto the rough concrete. She looks up and notices she is on Main Street and no longer in the school's open field. She looks around, and it still appears everything is paused in time.

The ache from the fall sets in. The palms of her hands burn with scrapes. She clenches her hands close to her body, trying to tolerate the pain. Friend reaches out his hand to help her up, but Abby rejects the offer. Friend sighs and walks away carelessly. He ends up by the cleaner's shop right next to the alley where she fell earlier that morning. As he enters, the chimes above the door ring cheerily.

She glances over her shoulder at the sound of approaching footsteps in the distance. Her eyes widen as she sees herself making a turn on Main Street from this morning. Abby hears chimes again; this time, it's Mr. Carter walking out of the cleaners. Strolling down Main Street, he checks himself out, fixing his hat and tightening his tie in the store's front windows and parked cars' windshields. The other Abby continues to run down the street. She hears Friend's growls and clicks as he emerges out of the alley and pushes her toward the muddy puddle on the sidewalk. Abby sits motionless, watching everything unfold. Friend, standing over Abby, holds a used and damaged journal. He reaches for her backpack pocket but instantly vanishes along with Mr. Carter and the other Abby. She begins to question what Friend may be concealing from her.

Before she can make sense of it all, she hears a loud noise coming from inside the cleaners. She walks in and sees the store is a mess, clothes tossed around the clothing racks and floor, like a bomb went off. The owner sits behind the counter with a tired face, leaning both elbows on the surface, oblivious of what's going on. It doesn't take her long to realize Friend has paused time again while he searches the racks for some clothes—Abby was wondering what his intentions were. Friend looks at Abby, he's standing tall with no blood on him, wearing a new suit like the one Mr. Carter is wearing.

Friend continues rummaging through more clothes. When he turns to Abby wearing a large sun hat wrapped in a pink ribbon with an artificial sunflower on its side, he menacingly curls his fingers, cracking a creepy smile while trying to break the tension between them.

"Do you think this is all a game?" Abby asks.

He nods yes. Friend removes the hat then scouts for something more useful.

Abby breaks the silence. "So, your name is Friend, right? Who gave you that name?"

He whimpers again and points at Abby.

"But I don't know you," she says, confused.

Friend becomes stressed, breathing heavily, pointing, and tapping the side of his head rapidly.

Abby replies, "I don't remember. Maybe you have the wrong person?"

He shakes his finger side to side, gesturing no, and points at Abby's necklace.

"How did we get here?"

He points to his head.

Abby points to outside. "Out there, I was pushed by you. Why?"

He points at the suit.

"Okay?"

He leans over the counter, growling clicks; he seems annoyed at the question. He walks to the back of the shop where the pile of clothes is. He picks up an umbrella, clutching it tight and staring down at the floor, zoned out.

Suddenly, Abby hears heavy rain and thunder in the distance coming from outside. "What are you doing, and what are you trying to show me?" Abby asks as she pins herself up against the entrance door. To answer her question, he tosses the umbrella to her, and she catches it.

In a blink, she is outside but somewhere she doesn't recognize. She looks around. A house sits before her, the yard unkept and filled with rusted car parts and a kid's jungle gym set. There are dense woods behind the home. A flash of lightning strikes in the sky, and the rain begins to pour. Headlights point toward the home, followed by the sound of a car pulling into the driveway, alerting Abby. She opens up her umbrella and listens as she hears yelling from inside. A man and a woman argue, but she can't make out what is being said. Abby crouches down, hugging the exterior of the house with the umbrella covering her head. She slowly but carefully gets halfway around the house, pinning herself next to the steps of the back entrance, trying to get close enough to make out what the man and woman are talking about.

"She can't stay here anymore," the man says. "She has stayed long enough."

"She's not going anywhere. She needs a place to stay," the woman replies.

"A place…it sounds like she can figure that out for herself. Haven't you noticed that thing is getting closer? The feeling we are always being watched…that man with the umbrella stands outside every time I'm home."

"Haven't you noticed it happens when you are drunk and yell like what you're doing right now? I asked her, and she said it's to protect her."

"If that's the case, then why are we taking care of her for this…thing?"

As the voices move around in the house, Abby bumps into a rusty, pink tricycle with a broken wheel, making a loud noise.

"What was that?" the angry man says.

Her necklace begins to glow, and heavy footsteps hastily walk toward the back door. She has no time to run away and no idea where to go. The necklace glows even brighter, so she wraps a hand around the crystal, franticly trying to hide its light. The handle of the back door turns and cracks opens. Abby tries to hide under the umbrella, pinning her body up against the back steps, fighting back her panic.

A flash of lightning burns brightly and stays so. The rain becomes sharply quiet. Abby stays hidden, afraid to move from under the umbrella. A long pause of silence and the lightning still stuck in the same place, Abby knows Friend stopped time for her. She peeks out and sees Friend at the end of the yard, hiding behind an old, rusty shed with holes in it. She gets the courage to remove the umbrella from her head. She still doesn't know why she is here and doesn't know what is to come. Friend's tall silhouette begins waving Abby over to him, but she has had enough.

"I want to go home," she insists.

Friend points at the house as if he is telling her to watch.

"I don't want to be here, so please take me home."

Friend is still pointing at the house, then at his head.

"No, I don't remember this. If that's why we're here, I don't know how to tell you that you might have the wrong person. Is this my past, and are they my parents?"

Abby turns around. The yelling man was seconds away from noticing her with his foot sticking out the door and his shadowed head looking down at her hiding spot. The man clenches the door handle tight with rage. She backs away and heads toward the kitchen window and sees the woman, sitting at a table. She surveys the condition of the home: the old wallpaper peeling off the unkept walls, roaches crawling on the table, glass bottles cluttering every surface, and boxes of cigarettes littering the floor with other garbage.

Friend clicks and groans, getting Abby's attention. She agrees she doesn't want to get caught. Abby runs to Friend, watching her step, making sure not to trip. Time resumes to the heavy torrential rain as it bounces off Abby's umbrella. She tries to stay dry as she makes her way behind the shed. Friend puts his hand onto Abby's head, forcing her to crouch to hide. He grunts with a deep, gurgle-like click, looking at the house with aggression and beginning to breathe deeper. Abby's necklace glows again, and he grabs it, hiding the light.

The back door swings open, but it is too dark to see the man's face; all Abby can see is the man has a glass bottle in his hand. "Show yourself. I know you're out there!" the man yells at the yard, stumbling through his intoxication, holding the door handle for stability. "Show yourself!"

A noise comes from the inside of the house. "Now go!" the woman's voice yells, but the man is too drunk to react. Suddenly, a small silhouette appears, pushing past the man.

"Come here, girl!" But the small girl does not listen. It is too dark for Abby to see the little girl clearly, but a glow of light blue hangs around the silhouette's neck. The man raises his voice at the girl as she runs into the junkyard field. "Get back here right now or I will—" A flash of lightning illuminates the world, revealing the girl's identity. It's Abby but younger, around eleven years old, and she looks a little different.

She has no recollection of this event ever happening in her life.

Her younger self runs into the center of the field, panting and shaking with adrenaline. She takes in a deep breath, yelling out,

"Friend!" Her necklace glows, revealing the dirt on her face and how unkept she looks.

"Abby, get back here!" the man yells at her.

She doesn't listen. "Friend!" she yells again as the man stumbles to her. Abby's necklace glows brighter and brighter, lifting straight out in front of her. She inhales, ready to yell one more time, but her arm is jerked above her head.

"What did I tell you about talking to your monster friend?!"

Young Abby starts to kick and scream, "No, no, no," as she fights to stay outside. The man attempts to pull her back inside. She loses her footing, sliding on the thick, slippery mud as she tries with all her might to stay outside.

A heavy, deep groan comes from behind young Abby and the man, and Friend appears, panting in rage over the man touching young Abby. This Friend is wearing a different suit: checkered blazer and matching pants with a white button-down shirt, a navy blue tie, and a fedora. She stops struggling, and the man bumps into Friend and lets go of young Abby. He turns around, looking up at Friend's featureless face. The man is too shocked to move. The other Friend picks up the man by his collar, lifting him to eye level. The man locks eyes with his intimidating hollow eye sockets that glow blue. He growls with clicks.

"Let me go, you monster!" he pleads in hysteria.

Young Abby is in shock as the other Friend raises the man higher, grasping him tighter while he struggles to break free. Friend's eyes and mouth glow brighter blue, opening his mouth wide and letting out an immense, growling roar of aggravation.

"Please...think about what you're doing because none of this is worth it. They let me stay in their home a lot longer than most. Let's face it, this wasn't meant to be. Please listen to me; he wasn't meaning to harm me. I forgive him, and I want you to do the same," Abby rants in desperation, hoping Friend will listen. Friend tightens his grip, and the man quickly starts to age, speeding through the remainder of his lifespan as he screams in agonizing pain.

The voice in her head begins to talk to present Abby. "Don't speak a single word or he will find out I am still around. I know this might be a lot to take in for you, and I also know you don't remember this, but I do. This is a very important moment in our timeline together. It must be hard to see how he used to do things, but we had rules we followed. Our story is too long to explain; for now, I will tell you this. We are not that different from each other. I also was looking for a new home after living multiple lives in multiple timelines, trying to fit in, but life always found a way to push me from a normal family. That was part of the plan. I will give you one piece of advice. Be strong; there is a lot to learn and dangers that lie ahead, and you will not survive if you don't think like Friend." The voice leaves her with more questions, like what it meant by "living multiple lives in multiple timelines."

Abby shakes her head, not understanding what it all means.

The other Friend makes a deep and terrifying roar, and his eye sockets glow bright blue at the man as he becomes too old and frail to move, reaching out in the direction of young Abby. "I am sorry…Izzy…" he says, taking deep breaths in between every word but not strong enough to speak them. Young Abby shuts her eyes tight, shedding her own tears, and looks away, knowing what is next to come. The man looks as if he is over one hundred years of age, emaciated, boney, wrinkly, and limp. Friend's fingers clench on the man's now fragile body, cracks spreading across his skull, then turning into dust.

Young Abby stands poised, clenching her teeth as she tries to fight back her tears. "I don't understand why you would do that." She stares at Friend, disappointed. "Izzy, the woman inside, helped me a lot. She gave me this address, and I think this is the key to help us out." Friend approaches Abby, leaning in for a hug. "No, you don't understand!" Abby tries to push Friend away while he leans her into his arms. Friend insists on comforting Abby. As distraught as Abby is, she finally accepts his embrace. She crams her face into the shoulder of his blazer, weeping. "I know this is not what you want, but this is what we must do before he comes. I know you can sense him. We need to lay low, and you need to control your rage. Do what is right and give back his life."

He groans deep within his clicks, disapproving her request to bring back the man's life. She slouches her shoulders downward, letting out a heavy sigh, "I understand." She says as Friend hugs her tight, displaying their true bond with each other as he snaps his fingers, then they vanish.

The present-day Abby and Friend, who watched everything unfold, remain hidden behind the run-down shed.

Abby is still in shock, losing her best friend and now this. Even if Friend could bring them back, she still cannot comprehend his reasoning or purpose for hurting them in the first place. She has no recollection of any of the events Friend has revealed to her so far. "I don't recall any of this. Why would I call you my friend if you hurt people?"

Friend is taken aback. What he thought were good intentions quickly backfires, and he begins to overanalyze his decisions. He reaches over to Abby's arm to show his apology but is denied.

"Don't touch me. Just bring me home."

His behavior becomes flustered as he clenches the sides of his head in frustration, fighting his own emotions.

Time shifts around them, altering their surroundings. The trees burn to ash, just like in her dreams. A loud, siren-like scream is heard from the other side of the shed, and the siding melts from the structure, half of the roof peeled away. The house is no longer there except for the foundation on which it once sat. The scream fades, followed by chattering teeth that give her chills.

"We need to go, *now*! Please, Friend, please, I don't think we're supposed to be here." Meteor-like pieces illuminate red portions of the smoky sky, catching fire on the way down to Earth. "Friend, let's go!" Taking Friend's hands off his head, she snaps him out of his panic and into reality, but it's too late. She can hear the creature. "Friend, let's go, we don't belong here. Come on. Bring me home."

Panic sets in. She can hear restless breathing and sniffing around, making a chattering, ticking sound while stomping the ground, sounding like it has more than one set of legs. The sniffing grows closer and closer to her. Its footsteps vibrate through the ground where she is hiding, then it stops moving. A pause of silence as she holds her breath. The creature sniffs around, then lets out a piercing screech, startling Abby as she holds her hands up to her ears. Friend puts his arms around Abby protectively. The creature pokes its flat snout around the shed, revealing its sharp teeth dripping saliva and chattering franticly.

Abby stifles a startled gasp, trying to back up, but Friend holds her tight. Her necklace glows with Friend gripping Abby tighter to him, enveloping her body in a warm, secure hug, and it feels normal, familiar, and safe, as if she has done this before, decreasing her worry. This feeling of protection and the sense of being wanted, she has never felt it in her life.

Friend puts his hand on Abby's chest. She holds on tightly to his hand, closing her eyes, then hears children laughing. She opens her eyes to her school hallway with Jennifer and Rachel standing before her.

CHAPTER THREE

The Voice

Time has shifted once again, as Abby is standing, holding her textbook tightly to her chest, back in school. Some students linger in the hall, trying to investigate as they walk toward the laughter. This is all too familiar for Abby as she glances at the clock and it is still too early for first period. She knows what to expect when Jennifer gives Rachel a look. Rachel reaches out with the letter in her hand, and Abby looks down at it and, with a firm voice, says, "Sorry, Rachel, I'm not taking that." She pushes the letter away as the students instigate, saying "Ooo!" as tension rises.

Jennifer shifts uncomfortably, bordering on embarrassed, as eyes rest on her to see what she will do next. "What are you scared of, Abby? Are you scared of what is inside, the truth of how everyone feels about you? How you don't have anyone in your life and you're just known as the dirty foster girl in this whole town? If one day you go missing, no one would care you're gone. You're nothing but a waste of life no one feels sorry for," Jennifer says.

Abby is not known to carry on an argument; it is not in her. She usually would just allow the verbal abuse to happen, but something has changed. All she can think about is the voice's advice to be strong and know there is a monster named Friend who is looking out for her. With that friendship, Abby has gained the confidence she needs to stand up for herself and face the obstacles that stand before her. "I am not scared of your little paper note, and I am definitely not scared of you either. Oh, and by the way, it's sad to see you fight so hard to make people like you."

More students crowd around like moths to a flame as some shout out, "Fight back!" Abby never knew how good it feels to stand up for herself. The feeling of empowerment tingles under her skin, exhilarating her confidence.

Jennifer flushes with embarrassment. "Rachel, give her the note," she tries to say discreetly, clenching her teeth to hide the movement of her mouth.

"But she doesn't want it," Rachel not-so-discreetly replies. Students erupt with laughter.

Abby starts to walk away, feeling the power of winning this battle.

"You have no friends!" Jennifer yells at Abby as a last effort to get back at her.

All the students in the hall pause in silence, waiting for Abby to say something. She stops walking and stands in the center of the hallway. "I do have a friend; unlike you, I don't have to beg." And she continues to walk down the hall.

Abby pushes the school entrance doors while Jennifer lashes out, "Your friend is imaginary." Allowing Jennifer to get the last word, Abby feels like she won this battle.

The doors close behind Abby, and she ditches school for the first time. She sighs, relieved to leave, not wanting to experience another day in school. She pauses on the front steps and takes a second to herself, re-imagining when the town was in flames and thinking to herself all the questions she has still not answered. Morgantown burnt to fire and snowy ash, the blue dome over the courtyard, and Friend being gravely injured.

"Friend, where are you?" she says softly and worriedly looks down at her necklace. She directs her attention back to Court Square, remembering the blue dome that had spared it from destruction. The bell rings for first period, shaking her out of her deep thinking. She ignores the bells and walks away from school, intending to find out where Friend may have gone.

She walks down Main Street to the cleaners and looks inside; Mr. Carter is flailing his arms, screaming at the owner inside and not wearing the suit she saw him in this morning. She can read his lips saying, "Where is my suit?!"

The owner shrugs his shoulders, not for the first time, yelling, "I don't know!"

Abby is aware of why it is missing but not sure why Friend needs to wear a suit. She looks in the dark alley, seeing if Friend is there. A few steps forward and an overwhelming odor of rot comes over her. She glances around, covering her nose, and sees a bloody handprint on the side of the dumpster. By the size of the handprint, it has to be Friend. There are feathers and bird carcasses littered throughout the alley. She takes a step and stumbles over one of the carcasses. She tries hard to hold her breath but fails, and she can't proceed any farther because of the smell of death.

She backs away and takes in a deep breath. "Where are you?" She sighs, checking her necklace anxiously, waiting for it to glow, but nothing happens. Abby continues down Main Street, wondering where he would be. Her mind keeps straying back to the dome and the fire. If that is what's yet to come, she needs to head to Court Square to find Friend or any clues—she definitely can't go home yet without getting in trouble with Cece for ditching school.

In Court Square, everything seems to look normal. She always feels like she is at peace with herself here. Off at the end, there is a courthouse with large pillars on either side of the entrance, showing power and authority. A large statue stands in the middle of the courtyard. Cobblestone surrounds the area in a circle, benches and hedges hugging up against the bushes along the perimeter, looking up at the statue. The marble sculpture depicts a woman holding up one arm, saluting with her eyes covered by her hat while the other arm is holding a pistol at her side. On the base of the statue, there is a plaque that reads, "For the honor and bravery. Strength and courage. For those who fall for us in the secret war."

Abby admires the statue, always wanting to be like the words written about it. She always had a personal connection to it as a role model, and it always comforted her every time she would sit on her favorite bench and visit with Ping. Abby thinks of Ping, sad he is gone and not yet having the chance to think back at all the times they had together. Every time Abby was upset, Ping would meet her at the park bench and listen to all of her problems. He was always there for her, as if he knew when she needed him the most.

She walks over to the benches to sit. She reads the words on the statue, "Bravery…strength…and courage." It makes her think about the voice. She feels different ever since Friend came into her life, like she has lost a part of herself and doesn't know why. Leaning back with her head up to the sky, she lets the sun warm her up in the cool fall weather.

As soon as Abby pushes back her head, she hears flapping wings getting close to her. At first, she pays no mind to it. She opens one eye, looking down, and can't believe what she is witnessing.

"Ping, is that you?" she says, happy but confused at the disheveled pigeon at her feet. She thought she would never see him again. "Didn't you…did Friend bring you? He must have brought you back since, at this time, you were alive. This is getting confusing." Ping just looks at Abby, ready to be there for her. "You have no idea what happened. I was here, but then I was somewhere else. That monster in the woods, he was showing me a place I don't remember. He says his name is Friend and I named him that, but I don't remember either. However, he showed me proof. But why now, why come find me now?" Abby looks down at Ping, who's preening his patchy feathers. She holds her necklace, hoping for a sign, but nothing.

A man sitting nearby catches her attention. His clothes are dirty with holes in them, and pigeons flock all around him. She has never seen this man before, and he appears to be homeless. One of his eyes is crooked, and he has one tooth sticking out. He violently rocks back and forth, rubbing his legs while staring at Abby. She tries not to look at him. It is hard not to, yet no passersby spare him a glance.

"The monster is back. Tell your friends and family to run before it kills us all." The man makes a clicking noise with his mouth. The same sound Friend makes. Abby looks away, afraid of the man's gaze on her. "Kill, kill, kill! And poof, we are all gone, right, girl? Your friend is protecting you and killing the rest of us... You know what I'm talking about, right, girl? You remember." An uneasy laughter comes from him. Ping flies away, leaving Abby alone and uncomfortable as he intently stares at her. "The end is near!" he yells and ticks like Friend while laughing to himself as she leaves the courtyard. Disturbed by his words, Abby walks through Morgantown; all she can do is rethink what that man said.

The voice comes back. "Friend is trying to see if you remember anything, and from the looks of it, you don't."

Abby rolls her eyes. "Oh, look, you're back. Maybe you should tell me instead of putting me through all of this, whatever this is? Why don't we start off with a name? Maybe it will help me remember."

"My name is Abigail, but he can't be aware you know my name."

Somehow, learning the voice in her head has the same name as her is the least of her problems, and she tucks it away for another time. "Why are you so worried about him? Is he bad?" Abby asks.

"No, not at all. He is one of the good ones—"

"So you're saying there are more like him?"

"With powers. Listen, Abby, if you really want me to walk you through what is going on, you need to let me speak. Friend is good, even if he kills. That's a part of his nature to him; only the purist survives, and that's a story all in itself. You see…how can I explain this and trust you won't say anything?"

"I promise I won't."

With a heavy sigh, Abigail continues, "Okay…Friend and I go back far. He was more than my friend; he was like a parent to me. He taught me all I know about his powers and what he calls home. That necklace you are wearing gives you his powers. He harvests his powers into what's important to him; otherwise, if he uses too much, he can lose all his strength. That's why he needed you to heal his wound. He gains back his powers when he feeds, like what he did to that little friend of yours, Ping—I would have given him a different name, but that's just me.

"Friend came from a different planet and, by mistake, came to Earth. He calls his planet Purity, located far away from here. We tried to find it, and we did, but we had no way of getting there without…"

"Without what?"

"It's better if you read about it. There's a part of town I bet you didn't know was around. It's just up the street."

Abby follows her directions, and on the corner is the old Morgantown Library, run down with the shingles falling off and every window cracked or broken. The library is covered in ivy and tall grass as Mother Nature engulfs the property. "I knew this was here, but it was always condemned. I never went inside."

"This was always known to be forgotten. You need to start to look at the bigger image. Friend would want you to remember this."

Before Abby can say a word, a wave of blue spreads before her, time shifting from the present to the past, back when the library was clean and open. She walks up the gravel pathway leading to the entrance, and she rests her hand on the library's antiquated wooden doors, rubbing against the grain. A small sign reads, "Open." Pushing on the brass handle, she enters the library. The overbearing smell of old books brings back memories of her childhood. She takes a couple of steps in, gleaning a layout of the surroundings.

There are two levels in the library. On the large main floor, there are bookshelves upon bookshelves occupied by a wide array of books and carts filled with more books that still need sorting into their proper genres. A tall ladder leans on one of the shelves, coated with a layer of dust. Most of the antique tables on the main floor are purposed for reading, but some hold PC processors and printers.

As Abby scans to her right, she notices a tall librarian's desk near the staircase. The stairs lead to a loft on the second floor that overlooks the main floor. Behind the desk sits a petite, elderly woman, who is wearing an Irish wool cardigan with her hair in a low bun, a faux pearl-beaded necklace, and cat eyeglasses with a chain attached. Before Abby can say a word, the old lady walks the opposite direction toward the shelves where she begins to sort and stamp a cart of library books.

She walks up to the librarian wearing a name tag reading, "Mrs. Baker."

"Hello, I'm hoping you can help me, Mrs. Baker. I'm trying to look for a book about monsters, ones from space…I think?"

"If you're looking for monsters, they'll be on the second floor all the way in the back. Just be careful; some books are old." Abby wastes no time rushing toward the staircase marked "Second Floor." Mrs. Baker loudly whispers back, "No running in the library."

Abby slows down, walking over to the far corner of the library where it is dimly lit. Dust and cobwebs cover the books and shelves. She blows on the spines, the dust kicking up into the air, becoming overbearing and choking her. A forceful "Shh!" comes from Mrs. Baker as Abby tries to muffle her cough, covering her nose and mouth while the dust clears.

She begins to scan the titles on the spine of the books, and time passes without her noticing, her search dragging on and on. "No...No...No...Come on," Abby whispers to herself. She climbs up an old bookshelf ladder to the higher shelves where all of the older books are but, after a thorough search, finds nothing. Just as she's about to give up, a sudden thud comes from the floor below her.

"Shh!" the librarian insists once again.

Abby descends the ladder to pick up the fallen book. It's much older than the others with yellowish-gray pages falling out of it and the title reading *The Unknown Universe*. She reaches down, but the book opens on its own, flipping through pages quickly, stopping on page 115 with the title "The Most Unknown," then slamming shut loudly.

"*Shh!*" comes even louder from Mrs. Baker.

Abby picks up the book, holding it close, and just before she turns around to leave, another book plops on the ground, but this one is much smaller, not as old but still aged. The book is off-green with a gold title, *The Magic of Time*. She picks it up, knowing these are clues to know more about Friend. She walks down to the main floor to check out the books.

"Oh, you're still here. I was just about to close," Mrs. Baker says, checking the slim watch on her wrist.

"Yeah. Wait, what time is it?"

"Oh, look at that. It's funny how time works. It's nine o'clock. No worries, did you find what you needed?" Mrs. Baker says with an uplifting smile.

"Yes, I did," Abby replies, putting the small book first on the table. The librarian opens *The Magic of Time*, stamping the inside of the book and handing it back to Abby. "And this one." She pushes the second book over, the librarian looking down at the thick, old volume, *The Most Unknown.*

Old and weathered Mrs. Baker loses color in her face, like she took her last breath, as she looks down at the damaged book with an expression of utmost horror. “Where did you find this book?”

Abby scrunches her eyebrows, confused. “Upstairs. It fell on the floor, and it was the book I was looking for, I guess.”

Mrs. Baker becomes flustered, panicking. “You guess! Girl, you can’t just guess on things like this. No, no, no…This book is not supposed to be here. How many times do I have to burn it for it to go away?” she says, spacing out over the title but quickly coming to, startling herself. “Okay, girl.” She tries to hold a smile, flipping over the front cover to stamp it.

As if freaking out about a book she tried to destroy on multiple occasions wasn’t weird enough, Mrs. Baker’s sudden calm unsettles Abby even more. Just like the homeless man in the courtyard, her eyes move at an alarming rate as she talks to herself. Abby reaches out to grab the book, but Mrs. Baker holds it in a tight grip, saying, “There are only some of us who remember, and this is not a chapter to turn over. Lives will be lost. My family doesn’t believe me; they think I am crazy! Just because I am getting older does not mean what I saw was not true. I warned them, but they do not listen. You remember, don’t you? Don’t you!”

Abby gets spooked, wrenching the book away from her. She makes a run to the exit door, but it closes shut. She tries to open it but no luck. Floorboards creak behind her under a large weight, followed by urgent sniffing.

“Oh no, you’re going to have to kill it!” Abigail franticly cries out, scaring Abby.

“What is it?”

“We call it a chatter, roaches from Friend’s side of the universe. It must be happening soon.”

"What's happening soon?"

"There is no time to explain. I need you to concentrate. We need to be quick and find a way to get on top of it. It has limited sight and uses its sense of smell and hearing. They seek out power users, like you and Friend."

The chatter sniffs the ground as it twists its head, listening for the subtlest of noises. Abby's knees wobble at her first clear view of the creature. Its bulbous body resembles that of a flea, only it towers over her on its four front legs and two rear cricket-like legs. As it swings its tiny head around, searching for her, its many spider-like eyes blink uselessly, confirming Abigail's claim about its poor vision. Her eyes are drawn to its protruding, drooling mouth, where its square teeth look capable of crushing her easily. No way can Abby take on this moose-sized flea.

The chatter remains completely still, hidden under the loft, just out of Mrs. Baker's sight. One of Abby's books slips from her hands and onto the ground. The chatter sharply faces in her direction with its many teeth bared. Without any hesitation, it charges her, screeching as it plows through tables, books, and chairs, knocking them over with its many legs.

Abigail pauses time around Mrs. Baker before she can witness the chatter charging. "Abby, you can't let Mrs. Baker see the chatter because it will disrupt the timeline. It's best for her to stay paused in time so she doesn't make a sound."

Abby leaves the book in front of the exit door as she dashes toward Mrs. Baker, ducking under her table as the chatter stops near the exit, waiting for the next sound. Abby peeks out from her hiding spot, trying to think of a way to get out.

Abigail loses her grasp on the power of the necklace, breaking Mrs. Baker free. Mrs. Baker leans forward, face-to-face with Abby. "I remember, and I will never forget. You did this to all of us. The portal will open, and doom will follow."

Abby slaps a hand over Mrs. Baker's mouth, trying to muffle her rant, but the librarian yells out before Abigail returns her to her frozen state in time. It's too late; they caught the chatter's attention.

It looks over, and Abby knows it'll charge in her direction, but she doesn't want it to hurt Mrs. Baker. She picks up an old, brass stapler lying on the ground and chucks it to the other side of the library, diverting the chatter's destructive path away from her.

Abby makes a run to the exit, but Abigail lashes out, "You can't leave. You must get rid of the chatter yourself. If you leave, Mrs. Baker will be the next one on its menu, trust me. Quietly run up the stairs and pick up some books for a trap." She listens to Abigail's demands, making her way up the stairs on tiptoe and grabbing some books. She leans over the bannister, looking down at the chatter trying to sniff out where she is. "Okay, Abby, this is what I want you to do: I want you to drop the books right over the edge to grab the chatter's attention. When it is beneath you, I want you to jump over the bannister and onto its back."

"You're crazy! I'm not doing that," Abby hisses.

"Listen, I'll help you when you're on its back. We need to do this now or the timeline will crash."

With the timeline in jeopardy, Abby has no choice but to gather her conviction, drop the books, and watch them fall, making a loud bang as dust explodes off the books and unkept floors. The noise echoes throughout the library. The chatter runs to the books, charging through anything in its path, and stops underneath her. Abby hesitates to take a deep breath before leaping over the banister and falling on top of the creature. The chatter screams, startled, as Abby sits between its head and bulbous body, and it bucks to shake her off. She clenches her legs together around his head, holding on for her life.

Abigail gives her instructions. "Place your hand on its head and try to concentrate and listen to my voice. I need you to relax.

Imagine the journey the chatter took to come here. Make it a timeline and try to see the truth."

Abby places her hands on its head, trying to concentrate. With her eyes closed, her necklace and palms begin to glow as she focuses on her task. Abby can see its timeline on a moon overlooking a large planet, a red beam of light coming from its surface, lighting up the dark, dead space. Portals litter the moon's surface with hundreds of chatters entering them.

"Concentrate!" Abigail says in a distant echo, reminding Abby.

She turns to see a large and powerful creature's silhouette standing on top of a hill, looking down on Abby, the chatters, and the portals. He wears armor that shines from the red beam of light coming from the vast planet and a red cape that whips violently in the wind. He looks ominous and scary as he turns to lock eyes with Abby.

Then the creature speaks in a deep voice, "I will meet you soon and take over your planet to watch it burn. Remember my name, little one: Buru." He clenches his hands as small, bright, red pulses of electricity course through his arms and legs. Knees bent and arms raised in a fighting stance, he punches the air, and his energy shoots out as a bolt of lightning, heading right toward her.

The ground drops beneath her just as the bolt of lightning reaches her, and she's back in the library, falling as the chatter turns to dust beneath her. She hits the ground hard. With fear running through her, she gets right up, running to the exit and grabbing her books along the way. She whips open the heavy, wooden doors and sprints off the property, turning around to find it back to the way it was, but one thing has changed: day has faded to night.

One of Cece's few rules: be home before dark. Abby starts to run, hoping to make it home, but her hefty backpack is slowing her down.

Abby and Cece don't get along as well as they should. Cece always keeps her distance, never getting too close, showing no signs of love or having any fun. Instead, she cuts through Abby's crap with a poker face, and she always sticks to her rules. She can be blunt and forthright, even if her words are harsh, but Abby knows her tough love comes with good intentions.

Abby finally gets home, but it's much later than her normal curfew. "Can't you do something about this? Change the time or something with your powers? Hello, Abigail?" Abby says, hoping for a response but nothing. Heavy with dread, she walks up the steps to the front door and takes in a deep breath.

She reaches for the doorknob, but it whips open before she can get to it. Cece is standing, disgruntled, on the other side. A petite, older woman with a hunchback, she usually wears a long, knitted cardigan with a scoop neck t-shirt and straight leg trousers. A navy, cotton bandana covers her head, and thick-framed glasses magnify her large eyes. She may appear kind, but she had a frowned look that proved otherwise.

She looks at Abby with her usual poker face and stern brows, not saying a word. Silently, she steps off to the side, leaving space for Abby to walk through.

She enters, tension and awkward silence suffocating the air. She doesn't know what to say or even how to explain why she is late. Abby turns around. "I'm—"

"Yes, you're late. Look outside; you can get hurt or worse at times like this."

"I was at school, and I was study—"

"Oh, yes, school and studying…yes, I see, and you were there all day, I'm guessing. You break my rule, and now you lie to me, all in one day. That's not the Abby I know." Abby's never heard Cece this mad before or this concerned. She never raises her voice like this. Cece points her finger at Abby. "No more of these lies, okay? Do you understand me?"

Abby nods her head in shock, saying, "Sorry, Cece. I mean it."

"Okay, now go. Dinner has gotten cold." Abby drops her backpack by the front door. Cece sits down at the table and points at the cold beef stew. "Eat," she says. Abby settles down at the other end of the table and begins to eat. The awkward silence fills the room as they sit, the only sound is Abby's spoon hitting the sides of her bowl. Then Cece slides across the table a folder with a sticker on the top that reads, "Potential Adoptees." Abby knows exactly what this folder really is. She begins to replay the common scenario in her head when she looks down at the table. Every single potential home thus far has not been what she envisioned. She often found herself running away from those families because she felt as though she didn't belong, resulting in her being returned to Cece.

Cece would always get angry at Abby, saying, "You really messed it up this time," or something along the lines of, "I'm not keeping you forever." She always reminded Abby she would not adopt her, but she never knew why. To her, it didn't make any sense. With all the years she has lived with Cece, it was just a sense of familiarity. Although Abby never knew anything about her personally.

"They're coming this week, and you're going to be here when they—"

"No," Abby cuts Cece off. "Oh, I mean, no one…umm…told me what happened to my real parents." Trying to play off her rude disruption, Abby lowers her tone, avoiding any more conflict.

With a straight face, Cece replies, "Some people just don't know how to be responsible. It's that simple."

Abby thinks back to when Friend brought her to the yard and how she saw herself with what her family could be, putting two and two together. "So they didn't die?"

"Girl, this wasn't a concern before, so why is it a concern now?" Standing, Cece walks away to her room.

Abby stays quiet, knowing the conversation is not going to come to a resolution. She opens the folder with the paperwork and pictures of the couple clipped to it. They're younger than what Abby expected, smiling happily. The woman has her arms wrapped around the man, and her tight, curly hair blocks half of her face as she tries to get into the photo. The man is skinny with short hair, big ears, and a large smile on his face. It's a much different photo than the others; they look fun and happy, and it doesn't feel fake or forced, making her smile back at the photo.

She zones out on the picture until she dozes off on the table, exhausted from her adventure. Lifting her head abruptly, she gets startled out of her sleep. She looks out the window and sees the first rays of sunrise poking over the hillside.

"Abby, can I ask you a question?" Abigail says. "Why do you think those people Friend showed you were your family?"

Abby rolls her eyes to the sound of her voice, getting up from the table and plodding to her room. She responds, "Ugh, why do you come and go whenever you please?"

"You know those weren't your parents, don't you?"

"I don't know. I thought I would give it a shot. It's a question I've never gotten answered."

"From someone who has jumped through time, sometimes, it's best to leave events that already happened in the past. When you change the past, you change the future, like the butterfly effect. One day, you will learn of your past, but live the life you have now. Even though living is dreadful, timelines aren't, so let's not mess with them."

"Who told you that?"

"Friend, and he taught me everything I know."

"You can understand him?"

"Yes, not only can I understand his groans and clicks as a language, I can feel him through his powers."

"If he taught you everything you know and you know him better than I do, why don't you want him to know you're alive?"

Abigail sighs. "Because he had a mission and he chose saving me instead of finishing something that is so important to him. If he thinks I am dead, then there is no reason for him not to finish the mission. It's complicated."

"Then what does that have to do with me? It's so frustrating to know nothing and get droplets of answers from a sea of questions. And where is Friend anyway?"

"Friend is taking some time to prepare. There are some things I must be vague about because, if you know too much, he will think you will remember and break everything we are fighting for. When this is all over, I will tell you, so please be patient."

"How long will that take? Time is not on my side."

"From what I feel, not long. Time is tricky but predictable, another thing Friend told me. I have to go for now. He will come to you when he is ready, so while you wait, read the books."

"But wait—Rrrrr!" Abby yells out in frustration.

Abby looks at the time, reading 7:10 a.m. She rushes to get ready, not wanting to be late again. Before leaving, she pulls the two books from the library out of her backpack and rests them on her bed, not wanting the old books to go to school, afraid they will get damaged.

She walks out of her room and can smell bacon and eggs; she hears the sizzling and popping coming from the kitchen on the main floor. It's Cece cooking breakfast. As Abby walks down the hall, she notices Cece's bedroom door is opened. This is unusual since Cece has always been adamant no one can enter her bedroom. Abby looks around before swiftly walking into Cece's room.

As she enters, she notices the room décor and furniture is antique. The Victorian-style damask wallpaper is faded, the gray rug overdyed, and the ivory, lace drapes yellowed with age. The only item that doesn't look ancient is the vanity in the corner. While worn-looking, the rose-gold varnish and hand-painted flowers give off a youth Abby wouldn't have associated with Cece. The room is immaculate; no personal belongings are on display. This could be anyone's room.

Abby is determined to find any clues which may lead to some information about her parents but soon realizes this might be more challenging than she anticipated. She breathes in and exhales heavily, closing her eyes while trying to control the power within her necklace. Abby concentrates, listening to the sound of the morning birds and of breakfast being made in the kitchen beneath her. Her necklace illuminates. The surrounding sounds come to a complete stop. Abby opens her eyes in amazement, looking down at her necklace for confirmation of her success stopping time.

Searching for a folder, a photo, or anything that may shed light on her past, she scavenges through the room. She looks under the bed and in the closet. Still no clues, but that does not deter her. Sliding the dresser drawer open, she comes across a photo she has never seen before. It's of a time before Abby was a part of Cece's life. The photo shows Cece, much younger, almost unrecognizable except for her large glasses. Standing in front of the brownstone door, Cece is slouched over, wrapping her arms around a young girl. The little girl, pale in the face, wears a green bandana while the rest of her body is covered by a sign that reads, "1st Day of School." Abby's necklace flickers, then time returns to normal with the sounds resuming.

"Come now. Don't be late for school!" Cece says from downstairs, startling Abby.

She quickly puts the photo back in the drawer and softly closes it before exiting the room. She walks outside with the sun rising on time like every other day, everything back to the way it was without Friend or Abigail.

Some barking comes from the neighbor's yard—Mrs. Leland's dog, Roxy—and Abby jumps out of her skin as Roxy slams her face up against the fence, growling and showing her teeth. "No, Roxy, come. I am so sorry, Abby," Mrs. Leland says. "Roxy has not been the same since the other night. I don't know what's gotten into her. She was never like this." As Mrs. Leland holds back Roxy by her collar, the dog's eyes widen, death in her stare. Abby remembers the night Friend came through her window and hearing Roxy barking outside, leading Abby to investigate for more clues.

"Oh, it's okay. I just got a little scared, that's all. Do you remember that night when she started acting like this?"

"Yes, I do. She was barking her head off, and I had to drag her inside. Mrs. Stark from down the block called me late that night telling me she could hear her from down where she lives—" She pauses for a thoughtful second and smirks. "Now that I think of it, I remember putting her back inside where she kept on barking, but within minutes, she completely stopped. I guess she tired herself out. Roxy never acted like this before, especially now she's getting older. It's like a switch flipped in her head. She seems more anxious and wary of sudden noises in the house." Mrs. Leland sighs. "I do not let her out the house too often. I cannot keep dragging her. I am getting older, and my kids are not around to help me anymore. When my husband, Joe, went missing, I got Roxy to help my children cope—they'd always begged us for one—but now they've all moved out, and I'm the one left taking care of Roxy." Her eyes lose focus as memories consume her.

Abby breaks through the silence. "Did you see anything else?"

"Oh, no, I didn't. Why, did I miss something?"

Abby guesses everyone but herself remembers what truly happened; just what Friend wanted, for no one to remember. “No, I just thought maybe something spooked Roxy,” Abby tells Mrs. Leland so she doesn’t look suspicious or crazy.

“Oh, that’s sweet of you, looking out for Roxy. Maybe you’re right, maybe she did get spooked. Well then, have a nice day.”

“You too,” Abby replies, Roxy inches from ripping her face off, and heads to school.

She walks down Main Street as people hurry past each other and cars drive by on their way about their lives with everything seeming to be normal. Farther down, she peeks into the alleyway, surprised to see it cleaned from top to bottom, as if nothing ever happened. The alley had smelled of pure death with dead birds littering the ground and being so unbearable for her to make it through. Abby remembers accidentally stepping on one, crushing its fragile bones. She looks down at the ground and notices a dark outline of where the bird once was on the cement.

Suddenly, a side door opens into the alley with a fat chef slowly making his way out, panting and grumbling to himself, disgruntled about his job. He is dragging two large and very full trash bags to the dumpster.

“Mister!” Abby yells out to the chef, startling him.

“Woah, geez!” In mid-throw of the garbage bags, he stumbles back, tripping over himself, one hand grabbing the dumpster next to him and the other hand holding his chest. The chef looks down the alleyway and sees a little silhouette of Abby standing at the other end, waving at him to get his attention. “You can’t be doing that, little one. People like me at my age can die if they get startled like that,” he says as he’s panting heavily and being overly dramatic.

“I’m sorry. I wanted to ask you what happened to all the dead birds that were here?”

The chef looks confused, picking himself back up. "That's all you want to know? That's a weird question to ask anyone in an alley, and who cares? They're dead; it's not like we can go back in time and save them all."

"I might be able to."

"Yeah, okay, kid, whatever you say. All I know is, one day, this alley was nice and clean, and the next day, it was littered with dead birds. I don't know what can kill so many birds in a short time, but all I can think of is a pack of alley cats or something."

"Really, a pack of cats," she says, acting overly interested in his suggestion while fighting back a laugh.

The chef continues talking, "That's all I can think of, but by the time we noticed the smell, it was too late in the night to clean it up. So we left them there to clean the next morning, today, but coming into work, they were gone. What do they mean to you? Were you training them or something? It's not every day a little girl stops you to talk about dead birds."

"Oh, I was just curious, that's all. Maybe you're right; it could be a pack of cats," Abby says.

A pause lingers while the chef takes a long, dirty look. "Is that all you need to know? Come on, speak up. I have to get back to work."

"Yes, I'm so sorry for disturbing you."

He mumbles under his breath, disgruntled as Abby turns away and continues to walk to Morgantown High, still on time.

She climbs the school steps while students lounge all over the front lawn, waiting for the first bell to ring. As she walks by a group, they stop what they're doing and watch her pass. She can hear the chatter from behind her, "She's the one who snapped back at Jennifer," "What's her name," "That smelly foster girl," "I heard she walked right out of school," and "She skipped school?"

Abby keeps her gaze straight ahead, looking at the school and noticing a crowd of kids on the top of the steps. She quickly realizes they are waiting for her. The crowd breaks open, and Jennifer emerges from it. "I thought you were too cool for school," Jennifer snaps at her, shoving her back to the edge of the steps.

"Listen, Jennifer, I don't want to fight. I would just like to go inside. Please."

"You embarrassed me, Foster Trash."

"You embarrass me all the time," Abby snaps back.

Abby attempts to walk away, to get into the school. Jennifer puts up her arm, blocking Abby from leaving this time. Jennifer smiles menacingly. "So where is your friend you said you had? Oh, sorry, I meant to say imaginary friend since people like you are, well, freaks, and no one can love a freak like you! Look, who am I?"

The kids listening begin to laugh aloud as Jennifer mimics how Abby acts shy and clumsy, making her look ridiculous as some spectators laugh even louder. Jennifer's actions enlighten Abby to how people see her. She sniffles, looking down at the floor. "Please, Jennifer, can you move? I would like to go inside," Abby pleads.

"Look, I guess I hurt your feelings." Jennifer laughs by herself while some of the kids shift uncomfortably and begin to think she has gone too far as they watch Abby trying to fight back tears.

"Jennifer, just let her go inside. She isn't hurting anyone," Rachel says with some kids agreeing.

"If she wants to walk past me, she'll have to walk past me herself," Jennifer snaps at Rachel. With no hesitation, Abby swings at Jennifer, but she dodges. Abby goes for another shot, her hand raised, but someone grabs her arm.

"What do you think you're doing?" a familiar voice demands behind Abby. Turning her head, she sees Ms. Perez, the guidance counselor of the school.

"You belong in a crazy home, not a foster home," Jennifer says, getting in the last word while Abby tries to break away.

"That was toward you, Jennifer. What do you think you were doing?"

"Me?! Well, I was...she came at me."

"I highly doubt that. That's not something Abby would do, and I don't want to hear your lies. You have one week of detention, starting the end of today."

"But—"

"Jennifer, I don't want to hear it."

Jennifer walks away, disgruntled, as her friends follow, and the crowd disperses with the first bell ringing.

The grip on Abby's hand releases. Abby quickly turns around, seeing Ms. Perez as well as two stone-faced men standing in the distance. They are wearing uniforms, a suit with a long jacket and black sunglasses covering their eyes. To Abby, they look like they work for the government. Her mind races, afraid, not knowing if they are looking for Friend.

"Abby, is it okay if we have a word with you in my office? It's about something important," Ms. Perez says, sounding concerned, wrapping her arm around Abby as they walk into the school together, making Abby more worried when the stone-faced men follow. They make it to her office, shutting the door behind them.

"What is it? What's going on?"

"Nothing is wrong, Abby. This will only take a minute."

Abby is feeling more and more concerned. "I'm going to be late for class, and I have to go to my locker and get my books, then—"

"It won't take long, and I'll give you a pass for your first class."

Abby hesitates. "Uhh...okay?"

"You can sit right there." Abby tucks herself into the chair as the men tower over her. Ms. Perez opens a filing cabinet on the side of her desk, mumbling Abby's name as she looks for the file. "There you are." She pulls out an overfilled folder, stuffed with documents and paperwork of all different colors, making a thud on her office desk. "Okay, do you know why I asked you here?"

Abby shakes her head, not wanting to say anything.

"Well, yesterday, you were in school, then walked out, and we were concerned about how your classmates are treating you."

"As well as can be expected. Can I go?" Abby's heart races, getting more and more concerned about where this conversation is going.

Ms. Perez looks up at the men, waving one of them over. One steps forward, laying another folder on her desk. Abby's heart drops, thinking they have proof of Friend. "So, Abby, I wanted to ask you why you left school property so abruptly if class hadn't started yet?"

"I was at the old library to study."

"The old library? The one that's been closed for years?" Ms. Perez asks suspiciously. When Abby remains silent, she shakes her head with a sigh. "Whether you were studying or not, that's not a good excuse to just get up and leave."

She gets scared, having that uneasy feeling Ms. Perez knows something more. She doesn't know what to say. "Well, I...I..." No words come out as Abby shifts restlessly in her seat, her palms beginning to sweat.

"Abby, we know why you left school property."

"You do?"

"Yes, I do. And while I like what you did by walking away, you shouldn't have walked out of school...No, I would rather you find an adult like me to talk to. Listen, I know change is hard, but I think it's time to move on in your life with a family."

"A family—wait, what? Ooh! I mean, yes, it is." The people are not here for Friend; they're here for her and the potential family. Abby plays along, feeling the tension loosen in her back. "Yes, that's why I left."

Ms. Perez opens the small folder and shows Abby the same documents she saw last night but with a different picture. The couple look like they are out to eat, sitting at a restaurant table. The woman's face is not covered with her curly hair; she has a long face and large, green eyes and a broad smile. The man has slicked-back hair with a beard and freckles, also smiling. "Abby, you need to promise me you will be home when they come. They will be in Morgantown a couple of days from now. Can you please not run this time? I have a good feeling about this one." Ms. Perez points at the larger folder filled with papers and continues, "This is all there is to know about you—"

Abby cuts her off. "If that has everything to know about me, does it say how my real parents died?"

There is an awkward pause in the room. "Well, I mean, I can look, but how do you know your parents died?"

"I mean, um…just a hunch, I guess?"

"If I look for you, can you promise me to give these people a good shot?"

Abby quickly nods her head, propping herself up against the desk and failing at trying to not look too excited as she awaits the truth.

Ms. Perez opens the large folder, flipping to the back to the oldest documents about Abby. She starts tracing her finger on some pages as she flips over a couple of them. "That's strange," she says, leaving a long, quiet gap as she thinks and reads further.

"What's strange?" Abby replies, breaking the silence.

"Well, I'm sorry to say, nothing here says anything about your parents. All it says is you were registered here in Morgantown when you were seven. I'm sorry if that wasn't any help."

"It's okay; at least you looked for me," Abby says, sounding disappointed. She gets up out of her seat.

Ms. Perez stops Abby. "Before you leave, I have one more favor for you. I was meaning to give you the flyer yesterday, but you were not here. Tomorrow is the fall social, and I was really hoping for you to participate in it. I think it would be good for you to step out of your shell and socialize with some of the students before you leave."

Abby quickly realizes when Friend brought her back to school for the second time, everything that transpired before did not occur. Being traumatized by her head being dunked in the toilet, the video, being approached by Ms. Perez with the flyer, the talk with Mr. Booker, and the senior from the field. Relieved that some events no longer exist in anyone's memories, she can move on from the embarrassment.

"Thank you for taking the time for us to talk, and I'll be seeing you at the social. Remember in a couple of days you will be meeting your potential new family with your foster parent, Cecilia. I hear great things about this couple. Cecilia and I think they are the right ones for you. Between me and you, I think you'll fit right in."

Abby nods, having nothing to say as so many thoughts bounce around in her mind. She reaches down to pick her backpack off the floor, and as she swings it over her shoulder, it's much heavier than she remembered, and she slightly loses her balance. "Okay, bye, Ms. Perez." Abby walks over to the door where the two men in the suits stand off to the side so she can get by.

"Oh, Abby, you forgot your book."

"My book?" she mumbles to herself, confused as she turns, seeing Ms. Perez holding the small book, *The Magic of Time*. Her heart drops. Abby grabs the book from Ms. Perez. "Thank you." Desperate to get out of there, she turns and hastily makes her way out to the hallway.

Abby weaves through the halls, looking around and over her shoulder, making sure she's the only one. Taking a sharp right, away from her class and her locker, she finds a hallway bench and sits, making sure once more there is no one in sight. She opens her backpack, and it reveals the other book, *The Most Unknown*. Abby remembers keeping both books at home and in her room, leaving her to assume Friend did this. Looking at *The Magic of Time*, she notices red string sticking out of it that wasn't there before. She opens to the page and finds a bookmark on the other end of the string that says, "It's time to read," on the center of it.

The school bell rings, startling her. Slamming the book shut as students flood out into the hallway, she knows it must be a sign from Friend, but it's not the right time. She blends back into the crowd, ready for her next class, and as the second bell rings, she wonders where Friend can be.

CHAPTER FOUR

Fighting Memories

Back at the junkyard home where Abby and Friend last saw each other, Friend can hear groans and chattering noises from behind the shed as he holds Abby tight, upset while she begs they leave. A screech like a siren screams, snapping him to attention. It's a chatter. His mind is in a fog, not thinking of himself, as he puts his arm on her chest with the blue glow covering her, then vanishing, returning her back to school where she will be safe and leaving Friend all alone.

More shrieks and screams are heard off in the distance as more chatters respond to their brethren alerting them to the shed. Before Friend can even react, a chatter tackles him onto his back, face-to-face with the creature as it chatters its large, square teeth, saliva dripping onto Friend's face as he struggles to fight back. He slows down time as it's chattering its teeth, timing the opening and closing of its jaw, and when the second is just right, he sticks both of his hands into its mouth, holding it open. Time goes back to normal as the chatter tries to close its mouth, but Friend is too strong. It whips its head, trying to shake loose. He begins to force open its mouth as it screams in pain and for help until its jaw snaps. The chatter shrieks and screams as its lower jaw swings, disconnected and immobile.

In the distance, a herd of trampling footsteps threaten, rushing toward the screams. Friend knows he must silence the chatter. He grasps the yowling beast with glowing hands. He makes a fist and swings at it, striking its broken jaw, and the chatter disintegrates to dust, to nothingness.

A silence lingers for a moment as Friend concentrates on leaving this timeline and returning with Abby, but it's too late. Three more chatters appear from the charred woods. They stop suddenly in a row, sniffing the air and chattering their teeth, as if they are communicating to each other. Friend stays quiet and perfectly still as he hides behind the battered shed. He tries to use his powers to get away, but still no luck. One of the chatters peeks its head on the other side of the shed, sniffing; when it's looking the other way, Friend punches at its many eyes. As it inhales to scream for more chatters to come and attack, Friend disappears into thin air.

The chatter loses sight of him, exhaling its scream into the smoke-filled air, not ready to alert the others yet. When its guard is down, Friend reappears with a charred branch, one end still burning and as sharp as a dagger tip, and pierces one of its eyes, then disappears. It screams in sheer pain, stumbling over itself until falling to the ground, dead, but alerting the other two chatters.

They scatter over to the dead chatter's body, looking around but not seeing Friend, confused on how their companion died. They sniff the air, trying to smell where Friend is hiding, but he is too fast. He reappears next to the most off-guard chatter and punches its leg and head with a fatal blow, crushing its bones with a splintering crunch, and its limp body collapses as Friend disappears again.

A long pause stretches on with only one chatter left. It looks for Friend, not sounding its alarm, as it doesn't know where the danger is coming from. The final chatter sniffs around as it clicks its teeth and saliva drips from its mouth. It stops, turning its head as Friend appears. They stand face-to-face, snarling at each other. The chatter opens its mouth, building up air in its lungs, ready to scream out like an alarm for others to come, but before it can, Friend uses his powers, blinking from the left, then to the right, slicing its throat. Sounds of gargling come from it as it chokes on the blood pouring from its wound. It tries to scream, but nothing can come out. The chatter struggles, putting up one last fight before it falls, its legs curling into a ball, dead.

All three chatters are dead with not a single ounce of blood on his suit and tie. Friend straightens his suit before walking away without a sense of direction but knowing he needs to find a way out.

A sudden rush of pain erupts in his head. He falls to the ground, clutching his head and roaring as he glows blue. Abby's voice echoes within his skull. "You're my best friend. Together forever, no matter what. That's what friends are for. Whatever happens, you have to go home without me..." The words fade along with the pain. Friend looks at his surroundings, still in the fire and ash world where he feels trapped.

An old man's voice comes over Friend. "We did not train you like this. What do you think the Nobles would say if they knew you chose to protect a planet that's not yours? You shouldn't be so vulnerable to their plights." Blue, glowing outlines of footprints walk past Friend into the sweltering woods. The footprints are small, human, and the only person that comes to mind is Abby.

They start off slow with one foot leading the other. As Friend follows, the footprints begin to run, and Friend tries to keep up as Abby's voice rings in his head, "If things don't work out, leave me behind and don't ever look back. Don't ever look back. Don't ever look back." The words echo within his head, throbbing in pain, but his determination keeps him moving forward.

The older man's voice chimes in, "She said it herself: don't ever look back. But you did, and while you were gone, I watched her this whole time, and she doesn't remember. She lived a life without you, without having a single thought of you come across her mind. I know because I am the one who listens to her every day. You show her things from her timeline, and still, she does not remember. How much more time do you need to move on? Because you don't have much time left; *we* don't have much time left. Purity needs you more than ever. So the question really is, what do you want: Purity or this? Because she's gone, and she's not coming back."

The footprints stop abruptly down a pathway, then slowly disappear as their light fades. Friend collapses to his knees, destroyed. He struggles with his powers as memories bring him to past events. It acts like an illness, effecting his power of time.

He vanishes as he's forced back to a time he would rather forget.

A moment he cannot alter nor unsee. Friend's past life on Purity, his home planet.

Friend stands poised in front of two tall and thick doors, gold-plated with markings on their surface. The markings are written in Purity's language and read, "Purity's light shines by the Nobles and Gods." For Friend and the purest of Purity, the doors represent hope. They give a sense of security for all of those who live on the planet. On guard with his fist on his chest, Friend is ready to protect whatever is behind these doors.

The Elders, the oldest creatures who live on Purity, wrote of the three Gods who once ruled on Purity centuries ago. They wrote of a super sun that sustained their planet for many centuries until, one day, the super sun burnt out, and Purity's blue beam of light was born. As the purest tried to endure off Purity's light, the Gods worked alongside the Elders, creating portals in their quest to find a new habitable home. However, the Gods soon disappeared. The Elders claimed the Gods were still pursuing a new home for the purest, and the Nobles continued to rule Purity on behalf of the Gods to keep faith in, one day, finding a new home. Then famine and death took its toll, and the planet began to show its slow death.

Desperation took over as the Nobles went on a mission to search for a livable planet. While on their expedition, the Nobles found one that was rich and habitable. While it was ruled by unknown creatures, they had an established hierarchy and a community, and the Nobles quickly realized they were not going to be able to move to this planet right away. Instead, their leader gave them an offering as recognition of the Nobles great powers—the Nobles were unaware of these creatures' capabilities or what damage they could do to the universe as a whole.

The Nobles accepted the five infant creatures from the leader, each child representing a race of the unknown planet. They cast a spell that would make the creatures dormant for an extended period of time. They would awaken them once their powers were needed.

A message was sent by the unknown planet that initiated a peace treaty between the two planets to become one, but when the Nobles went through the portals to negotiate terms with the planet's leader, they never returned. The portal closed with the Nobles trapped on the other side.

With no ruler left on Purity, the Elders closed the doors to the throne room. They had no choice but to help rule their planet, as no one else was left. They vowed to stay mute about what happened to the Gods and the Nobles and led their community to believe the reason for their disappearance was to search for another planet.

The Elders were on a mission to learn about these unknown creatures and raise them to be a part of their empire. Many years pass with no sign of the Nobles, resulting in the spell to break, allowing the five creatures to grow up and be raised by the Elders. They called them the Five Purists, named by the Eldest Elder, the oldest Elder in Purity, separated by the ones that live on Purity because their blood was from somewhere much different than ours. Their names were Buru, Alma, Torz, Sora, and Rouk—Friend's name on Purity. The Elders raised the Five Purists to police, protect, and prosecute any creatures who threatened the planet and any purests who did not believe in Purity's light.

The five creatures did not understand how powerful and strong they were, and they were hindered from using their powers. The Five Purists were assigned responsibilities to sustain Purity's hope and faith from collapsing. Among Buru's tasks was the position of prosecutor, to cast away anyone who broke the ethics and rules of the planet. Once, those who doubted their faith or preached hatred to other purests in their community were sent to a trial where the Gods and Nobles decided their fate, but this was now the job of the Five Purists. The ones prosecuted would be convicted and placed on one of the four moons, stricken of their name. Buru had to perform these acts to honor Purity and its faith.

Centuries passed, hope dwindled, and Purity's rules were broken by the purists. Some of the Five Purists began using their forbidden powers for their own gain, soon realizing they had enough power to rule planet Purity.

Friend looks much different in his timeline, almost unrecognizable. He has eyes and a formed face with no scars marking his skin. He is wearing a thin, shiny chest plate, spiky shoulder pads, and a cloth banner wrapped around the side of his waist with a symbol of a beam of blue light on it. He holds a helmet at his side, ready to fight if needed.

The Eldest Elder walks over to Friend as more Elders follow. The creature is old and hunched over with eyes on the sides of his bulbous head, and the skin on the back of his head is weathered and worn with long, loose jowls. The Elders have short arms and three long, sharp-clawed fingers crossed over their short, stubby bodies, and they all wear robes wrapped around themselves like monks. Eight of them circle around Friend and begin to talk in whispers.

"What are we going to do about Buru? We should have banished him to the moon and stricken his name when we had the chance. Now he has a small group coming to take over the capital, and the truth will come out." The Eldest fidgets, fear in his eyes. "We can't fight Buru. We are just the Elders, following the laws of Purity's light. What do you think we should do?" the leading Elder says as the others look up to Friend, waiting for his guidance.

He sighs with anger, grunting the name, "Buru."

A loud bang comes from outside. The Elders look around, scared. "This is impossible. Hurry, Elders, we must bring the others and purest out of harm's way." The other Elders whisper to each other.

One of the Elders shouts out, "To the catacombs, where else? But what are we going to do about Buru—"

"No, no, *no*!" the Eldest cuts him off. "We will bring him to the southern moon. Buru doesn't know it like we do, so he will starve or be eaten by the chatters where he belongs, but we must prepare. Hurry, Elders." One of the Elders opens their hand, fanning their fingers and curling their wrist, and a portal opens in front of them. All the Elders walk through, the Eldest Elder the last one to go. He turns to look back at Friend. "For Purity," he says, giving a smirk. Friend puts his fist on his chest as they nod at each other. The Eldest walks through the portal, leaving Friend on his own as he stands guard with his back to the large, gold doors.

Deep and heavy screams sound from outside as the capital is invaded, but he does not look or protect the ones in need. He is sworn to protect Purity's doors.

Buru's voice hisses from the shadows, "Brother, I am so disappointed in you. You waste your power to stand in front of a door of lies. You think behind those walls a color of light can save you or even the people of Purity? There are no Gods of Purity, and that beam of light is just an illusion. You see, the Elders know our people know that, but you didn't!" Friend gets pushed back, his body slammed against the doors. He lifts three feet off the floor, clutching at his throat, choking. "Look around, brother. Are any Gods scolding me for using my powers? You are a weak tool, brother, a tool with great potential. But you will always lose because I am Buru. I am true power and the true god of Purity!" A hand emerges from thin air and wraps around Friend's throat. The rest of Buru appears as Friend chokes in his grip, gasping for air.

Buru is massive compared to Friend. His sharp, jagged, rotten teeth have a stench that is suffocating. As Buru grips Friend, the black, crystal spikes on his armor, in varying sizes, dig into him.

Buru looks into Friend's eyes. "Fight me. Show your true power or fight alongside me." Friend does not budge, resisting his offer. "I understand, brother," Buru snarls. "You are set in your ways." He throws him aside, away from the door. Friend gasps for air as Buru walks up to the doors, pausing before opening them. "I will show you the truth, the lies we lived." Buru grunts as he opens the doors. A bright light blazes inside, making Buru and Friend cover their eyes so they can adjust and see what's inside.

Friend gasps for air, gripping the ground. "So, you chose to go against our own brothers, Buru, killing them off one by one for your own greed? The Elders were right; power leads all to war." Friend gets up and charges at Buru. He counters, punching Friend in the ribs. The sound of bones breaking forces him to the floor, once more collapsing under Buru's power.

Buru laughs aloud, lifting Friend's head. "See, brother? No Gods hiding behind these doors, just a beam. An illusion making you not use your powers, making you weak. But we can take this planet and be the Nobles and the Gods of these people. There are a lot of us out there who gave up on Purity a long time ago." He twists Friend's head around to the open doors. "Does it look like anyone—Elders, Gods, or Nobles—has been in here?"

Friend looks inside and sees a pyramid-like structure shining a thin, narrow beam of light out of its center. Three clear lenses of varying sizes hang above the beam, starting from micro small, medium, to a huge plate, and every lens the light goes through makes the beam grow larger in size. Around the room, yellow banners droop from the walls, ripped and weathered, with a red symbol on the front that is much different than Buru's. In the back of the empty room are steps leading to four Noble chairs, and a second platform leading to three more chairs, empty and covered in webs and dust, as if no one has been in this room for a very long time.

Friend pants in pain, hiding his hand from Buru as he tries to heal his broken and battered ribs to fight back, but a sudden jolt pulses through his back. Buru's hand glows with light, shocking Friend into unconsciousness.

"It's pitiful to watch you fall," Buru says as he places his foot on Friend's back, applying immense pressure. "It's even more painful that you don't listen when I speak. I would never lie to you."

White light flashes forward to a different period in Friend's timeline. Sounds of shouting and Friend on an elevated stage, steps leading up to the platform. Friend is stripped of his armor, tied against a black, jagged-spiked crystal erupting from the grand stage. His head hangs forward, wearing a red burlap bag, blind to his surroundings. Friend takes in a deep breath of the stagnant air. Recollecting his thoughts, he attempts to release himself while whipping his body and arms, the chains restraining him clanking together, but inevitably fails.

Undertones are heard around him of what sounds like hundreds. Friend begins to recognize he is at the prosecution sector. There's no escaping this, and Friend feels defeated, accepting the inevitable.

Different races of purest creatures crowd together, chanting with words that are scattered, making it hard to hear what is truly being said. Some cheers are shut down by boos roaring.

One of the Elders walks up the steps slowly to the stand where Friend's head is bowed down, weak and defeated. The Elder lifts off the burlap sack, revealing Friend's face, still unscarred. He has small, black, baggy eyes under his low, heavy brow, two small holes as his nose with a thick layer of skin bridging over the top, and small ear holes on the side of his head. Friend's jaw protrudes out, showing his square teeth.

He looks around at the crowded arena, spectators looking down at him. The crowd begins to roar, divided in hate and excitement, as Buru emerges, walking up the stage. He lifts Friend's head. "Pity how you fall, and here we thought you were the strong one," he murmurs so only Friend can hear.

Another Elder walks up the steps to Buru, holding a jar of a green, gelatinous-like substance with a disappointed look, saddened by what Friend is going through.

Buru puts up his hand to the massive crowd, and a silence so quiet falls only Friend's heavy breathing can be heard. "We gather here today to remember how we all lived our lives in fear. How we worshipped stories and myths that manipulated us. We all stand on this amazing planet and moons of Purity, and we are not afraid anymore!"

The crowd roars with mixed emotions, some chanting, "Let him go!"

"Silence!" Buru snaps back at the crowd in rage, and the crowd quickly quiets down. "My brother Rouk chooses not to believe there is nothing behind those doors and nothing to the light that comes from it. I opened those doors—"

Everyone gasps. Even the two Elders lower their heads in disappointment.

Buru goes on, "I found nothing. No Gods, no Nobles, just an old, empty room and the beam of light we call Purity, but there is nothing pure about it. Isn't that right, brother?" Buru laughs at Friend, who mumbles under his breath. "What did you say? Speak up before I stricken you to the moons."

Friend speaks up so everyone can hear the deep groan and heaviness of his voice. "He speaks the truth. There are no Gods, no Nobles, but remnants of what was once the truth and markings of what was once habitual. Life as you know it will change and, for many, will end. Buru wants to be your god. He abuses his power and will use that to his advantage. He doesn't care about your lives—"

"I'll stop you right there, Rouk. It's sounding like you want to be the next god, but tell me this: what god can rule if they don't even use their power?"

"One who chooses not to abuse power to kill for truth. Traitor," he snaps back at Buru as he loses control of the crowd.

Finding out the truth of Buru's intentions, some shout for Friend to be released. "Let him go!" the audience cries out.

Buru yells for silence at the crowd, but they revolt more. "That's enough! I will not let you speak to me like this. I am Buru, and I will have my brother stricken to the southern moon where he will live till death. Elder, hand me his punishment!" The Elder holding the jar bows, lifting it up over his head and handing it to Buru. Friend knows what will happen next, puffing up his chest with pride. Buru walks up to him. "You will speak no names nor see your fate. You will be stricken to the southern moon where you will suffer as you watch Purity change under my command."

Friend locks eyes with Buru, unafraid. "Until we meet again."

Buru snarls, "No, brother, this will be your end." Buru pours the liquid out of the jar over Friend's head, his skin sizzling on contact. Steam rises from his face, making it hard for him to breathe.

Friend lets out a deep and blood-curdling scream. Buru unties him from the crystal; he hits the floor hard and quickly puts his hands over his face.

Buru points at the Eldest Elder. "You! I want you to bring him to the southern moon as a stricken, banished by our home planet. Do you hear me, Eldest Elder?"

The Eldest Elder stares, horror-struck, at Friend with his eyes growing large over the irreversible damage to his face. The Eldest puts his hands close together, spreads out his three fingers, and pushes his hands away from one another, creating a portal on the stage.

Steam still comes from Friend's face. He breathes heavily, grunting and whimpering. The crowd is quiet and in shock over what is evolving. Friend's hands glow over his face, healing it to get rid of the pain.

Buru looms over him, letting out a laugh. "Ha, ha! Doesn't it feel good to use your powers, time bender? The only one from our group who wouldn't use it until now. What a waste!" Buru kicks Friend into the portal with it quickly closing behind him.

Friend flies in midair through the portal, transporting him to the southern moon, falling on the fine, purple and gray sand. The moon is dark with soft sand and black, jagged rocks. Large hills in the distance are spotted with holes, openings to caves other stricken tried to live in. Friend holds his head and lies curled up in a ball, trying to heal his face but lacking the strength. Time quickens, sand collects on top of Friend. The moon darkens and lightens as it orbits around Purity, the beam of light shining bright. A cold wind whips through, bringing with it the feeling of emptiness. The planet rotates from day to night, and days stretch into weeks, into months, with the mound of sand growing on top of him, the sand glowing as he heals.

When time finally slows down, the pile of sand begins to glow. Friend emerges, sand slipping over his long limbs as he gets up. He lifts his hands to touch his face. The skin is scarred, forever marked by Buru, and he grunts, looking out to see the beam of light still aglow.

A portal opens behind him. The Eldest emerges, frightened. Friend turns around with his hands out, ready to fight. "Stricken, is that you? It's me, the Eldest. Do you remember me?"

Friend nods yes, as he is no longer able to speak due to his injury.

"The scars Buru gave you, you did not deserve this; no one other than Buru does. You were the only one who followed the rules." The Eldest Elder reaches his hand up to Friend's face, but Friend looks away, not wanting anything to do with him. "Do you know how long it has been since we last saw you? It's been thirty years, thirty long years with Buru killing and influencing our people, and it's been going on for far too long. We need your help. Use your power and fight him to the death and take back what's ours. We're desperate."

He can hear the desperation in the Eldest's voice. Friend faces the beaming light and sighs in disbelief.

The Eldest Elder continues, "I know you saw the emptiness in that room, but I promise they were in there, the Gods and Nobles together, but that was hundreds of years ago. You see, us Elders were banned from talking about what happened to them, just in case they came back, but…so much time has passed; we lost hope until we found you and the others from your group. There is so much to say, but it's hard to know where to start…so much sacrifice that happened." He sighs, following Friend's gaze to Purity.

"Long ago, the Gods vanished, and the four Nobles went looking for them with the Elders' help, opening portals while they used their powers to fight their way through. But one day, we opened a portal, knowing we were close to getting back the Gods, but the portal closed with the Nobles inside. They knew how to open the portal, but they never did and never came back home. We did not want to tell the others in Purity, so we kept the doors closed, hoping, one day, they would come back. We had you and Buru guard and keep Purity relevant. The truth had to come out eventually but not like this. The Elders and I did not want this to happen. We knew you and Buru had powers and worried this would happen if your powers were used.

"Now your freedom..." The Eldest Elder heaves another sigh. "You can never come back unless you help us. The Elders and I are sorry about what happened to you, but we need you more than ever. We discussed about how to get you back, but we were scared with Buru and his men watching our every move. So when we felt your power when you woke, I came as fast as I could. We need you to take Buru out because we are running out of time. You see, Buru is going to take out Purity for his own good. He thinks you died a long time ago, and he is growing weak and losing control."

Friend clenches his fist tight, clicking and grunting, thinking about the lies and Buru.

"I need your help; we need your help. What do you say?"

Friend sighs, trying to hold his composure as he looks down at the Eldest Elder and puts his fist on his chest, a salute.

"Good...good! Listen, I don't have much time before my absence is discovered. When the eastern moon rotates three times around Purity's beam of light, I will meet you on top of that hill over there; I will come to you with a portal to bring you back home on the steps of Purity. We are in the works of getting our people who still believe together to fight and take down Buru."

Friend nods with a stern look.

"I'm sorry for what happened." A portal opens, and the Eldest Elder gives a final look at Friend's face, opening his mouth, as if wanting to say more, but holds himself back. He turns and walks into the portal, leaving Friend alone once again.

Wind blows through the barren landscape as he looks up at the caves. He crouches, picking up a handful of purple sand and watching the fine grains run through his fingers. He's tired of feeling alone. Friend flicks his wrists with power and energy running through his hands, vanishing to the top of the hill, ready to train as the image fades to the next memories.

He stands alone on top of the sand dune, perched on the edge of the black, jagged rocks to wait for the Eldest to open the portal. He looks up at the starlit sky and at the eastern moon above, making its final rotation and casting its shadow over the beam of light. Friend waits, trained and eager to leave but even more eager to fight for revenge over what Buru did to him.

More time passes and still nothing. Friend worries no one is coming to get him.

"Come on, we don't have much time!" a voice says from behind him where the portal opens, and through it, one of the Elders waves him on. With no hesitation, he runs through the portal, ready to fight.

He comes out the other side in front of the entrance steps to Purity's beam and looks up at the tall building where he once guarded. Blood runs down the steps as wide-eyed and small-headed purests fight amongst each other. Chatters outfitted in armor charge through bodies, barely tamed as they rip apart and trample others beneath them. Buru's army of red and black gear clashes against Purity's blue and gold.

Friend is stunned to see how time has changed his home, falling apart at the seams. Some soldiers stop fighting, staring at

Friend with open-mouthed amazement. He looks back at them, giving a nod as they put their fists on their chest, showing they are on his side. Friend turns back to the stairs, knowing Buru is up there to take out Purity's light. He lifts up his glowing hand before closing it in a fist, ready to show his true power.

He runs up the steps, Buru's soldiers meeting him with black-tipped spears and lunging at his chest. Moving out of the way just in time, he grabs the soldier's face and cracks his skull, his body turning to dust. All that remains is the helmet the rebel was wearing. Friend drops it onto the pile of ash.

Allies in blue armor stop to look on in shock. One of Buru's men tries to attack Friend from behind, but he is too fast. As the purest rebel lunges, Friend vanishes and reappears behind him, hand through his chest, and lifts the soldier up in the air as he screams. More fighters pause their fighting. As the soldier screams louder, Friend vanishes again, ripping the man from the inside, and silence falls over the scene. Friend reappears, covered in blood, and soldiers salute and kneel in surrender to him with one saying aloud, "The shadows speak truth. Rouk, our savior, comes back from the stricken moon, using his forbidden powers to defeat Buru."

A loud rumble and crack come from the building, shaking the ground beneath their feet. Thick cracks race across the front of the tower, loosening a chunk of rubble onto the fighters below. Friend puts out his hands, releasing a pulse of energy. The debris stops in time with a blue sphere around it. All fighting stops as everyone stares in shock and awe over Friend's display of power, holding the crumbled piece up so no one gets hurt. The fighters underneath run out of harm's way. More of Buru's rebels throw their spears to the ground and put their fists on their chests, surrendering. Friend lets go of the debris, and it free falls straight to the stairs below, exploding into chunks and engulfing the entrance in a cloud of dust.

A voice yells in the distance, "The legends speak truth. He lives!" Others respond with "Save Purity!" in a desperate cry of help, followed with more sounds of weapons, armor, and helmets being thrown on the steps. Fists on chests, soldiers pledge their lives to Friend, cheering, "The stricken lives! The stricken lives!"

Friend takes in the sight of his brethren cheering, feeling the power and hopefulness through them all, but he remembers this is not the time to cheer. Not yet. He points up the stairs with responses of readiness and convinces all those on the steps to follow and work together to take back what was once theirs. He uses his power to travel up the stairs and through the wall of dust in a blink, making a wave of air that pushes the dust off to the sides and shows his path. The soldiers from both sides team together, ready to fight Buru.

Behind the golden doors, Buru sits on the throne of the Nobles, looking down at the Elders preparing to remove Purity's blue crystal. "Where is the Eldest? He's late! I waited thirty years for this day to come," Buru says, slamming his fist on the arm of the chair.

The Elders don't say a word to Buru, ignoring his anger as they get ready to change Purity's beam of light. One Elder opens a bag and pulls out a transparent, deep red crystal while another presses down on the mini pyramid's hidden door, opening a secret latch to the blue crystal. The Elder hesitates to place the red crystal into the slot, feeling defeated and seeking hope, lost in his thoughts.

Buru's loud and demanding voice jostles him awake. "What are you waiting for? Do it already!"

One Elder speaks out, "Buru, this crystal and its light makes our planet prosperous and habitable. If you change it, all that is living will slowly and painfully die."

Buru sternly looks at the outspoken Elder, a deep laugh bursting out of him. "You and the other Elders breaking your own rules about speaking lies. You swore an oath to stay silent when these doors closed to keep your secrets quiet. You lied about the Nobles—Kreed, Ora, Zorc, Mia—and the Gods, and you lied about what was really behind these doors, all stories you wrote and fed us. So why should I believe you? If I did, I wouldn't be where I am today. The ruler of Purity with an army of soldiers who will kill for me as they chant, 'All hail, Buru, the one with true power!' Now do what you are told, or you will be banished."

The Elder places the red crystal into the slot with all of them shaking in fear. The beam flickers white for a brief second, then turns deep red, shooting up through the magnifiers into the sky. The red light casts an ominous and malevolent glow over the black, jagged city.

The city shakes as Buru laughs. "Yes, the color of my power to stoke fear within whomever faces me and my loyal army, the god's army. What a great day to live as rule—" Buru stops abruptly and sniffs the air. "I smell power. Strong power." Another sniff. "Brother!" Buru snarls as he sees Friend at the other end of the room.

Friend passes the Elders, pushing forward.

"It's been thirty years since I last saw you. Your unfaithfulness to your own brother, to your own…seems like you still don't get it, do you?" Buru vanishes from his chair, leaving traces of red electricity, and reappears face-to-face with Friend. "You are a scared monster, stricken by your own brother. How painful the truth sounds; hopefully, as painful as those scars I left on your face."

Friend flicks his wrist, power coursing through him, and takes a full swing at Buru. Small bolts of electricity flicker along Buru's skin as he moves swiftly, dodging Friend's fist and grabbing his head tight. Electricity pulses through Friend, shocking and stunning him. Buru throws him across the room, his body skipping across the ground like a stone on water and hitting the wall.

"You are still weak, brother."

Friend gets to his feet, assuming his own fighting stance, ready for more. Buru grunts with a smirk on his face.

"You still haven't learned your lesson now, have you?"

Friend stands still as a statue in his stance, waiting for Buru's first move. Buru's powers spark around his body in frustration.

He vanishes along with Friend in an epic battle of powers. They flash across every corner of the room. At times, it looks like Friend is losing while, other times, it's the complete opposite as flashes of blue and red light up the room. Friend struggles to get ahead. An epic fight of cat and mouse, Buru creates clones of himself, overwhelming Friend and draining his powers as he attacks one at a time, trying to find the real Buru.

Buru appears before the Nobles' thrones and laughs. "Come on, brother, what type of power is this? You're still too weak."

Friend appears, angry as he tries to prove he's strong enough. He vanishes, reappearing face-to-face with Buru and clutching his throat. Buru chokes out, "You still don't learn, do you?"

Buru copies Friend, grabbing Friend's throat and shocking him until he can't hold on any longer. Buru lifts him higher and flings Friend across the room as the Eldest Elder enters. The Elder gasps as Friend flies through the air, but he disappears and pops up before Buru, healed and with a hand back on his throat.

"Impressive," Buru says sarcastically, not the least bit concerned. He begins to laugh, startling Friend because the laughter comes from behind him. "Do you think I don't know what a time bender does? Do you honestly think I did not train for this very day?"

Before Friend can even turn around, a piercing sharp pain hits him in the back as he screams in agony. Friend looks down at the dagger tip of a war banner piercing through him. Buru's apparition disappears as the banner lifts, and Friend lets out a blood-curdling roar as he slides farther onto the pole. "See, brother? I have done my research on you. I have seen everything you can do."

Friend looks at the Eldest, who trembles in fear. Buru spins him around, tossing his body off the spike and onto the floor against the light beam's mechanism.

Buru laughs menacingly. "What I have learned is you can manipulate time, heal yourself with time, and look or be in other timelines of other lives. Your power makes it hard to kill you, but I have also looked in the Eldest's books, and it talks about that very thing. It takes a long time for you to charge your power, making you easy to catch."

Friend struggles to pick himself back up, barely able to hold his balance as Buru walks his way. Friend lets out a loud roar, power running through him as he heals his wound. Buru charges with the banner. Friend vanishes, reappearing on the top of the steps. Buru throws down the banner, charging up his power, walking, then sprinting toward Friend. Friend runs down the steps, ready to collide.

"Oh, no," the Eldest Elder says to himself, as he can see Buru's plan.

The Buru running toward Friend is another one of his illusions. His hand ever so slightly twitches. The Eldest can't let Friend fall for Buru's cheap blow that will end Friend and what remains of their home.

Making an impulsive decision, the Eldest opens a portal between the colliding forces, but he miscalculates and watches in horror as Friend enters the portal first instead of Buru. The Eldest Elder yells out, "No!" as the portal closes, leaving the enemy to destroy Purity and sending Friend to a whole new world, a world different from their own.

His new home, Earth.

Friend comes to, out of his memories and past nightmare timelines. He looks at his surroundings, realizing he is in Morgantown in the alley on Main Street now. Night has fallen, and he's unaware what day it is. Friend's legs collapse beneath him. His powers are weak, and he needs a moment to gain his strength.

Friend feels defeated when, suddenly, he sees a large alley rat emerging from the dumpster with its oily-smelling fur, yellow teeth, and thick, deformed tail. It jumps off the bin, and in midair, it's snatched up in Friend's grip. As it squeals in pain, choking for air, its eyes bulge under the pressure before it begins to decay into his hands. Flesh and bone peel and fade away, leaving a slimy flesh jelly. Too weak to properly feed his power. Friend opens his hand and slaps the rat's remains onto the dumpster, leaving a bloody handprint.

Friend sighs heavily and clicks to himself in the alley, overwhelmed with emotions. A flash of lightning strikes, followed by pouring rain. He sighs once more, thinking just his luck as he is unable to pause time. He grabs a large cardboard box from the trash, using it to stay dry. He sits behind the dumpster and weeps, frightened for Abby's safety. His fear of abandoning her messes with his emotions, even though he doesn't know who he really is to her.

Ping appears, flying down the alleyway, swooping in to land on Friend's knee to get out of the rain. He wipes his beak on his dress pants. The old man's voice that sounds remarkably similar to the Eldest Elder's begins to speak. "We can't be playing this game, especially when Buru knows you're still here. You trained her well, but she lost it all. You tried bringing her back but ended up creating an alternate timeline where she doesn't know you and has all she's ever wanted: a home, a school, and a normal life. She's safe now. It's time to move on. I know it's hard for you, but it's better this way.

It will help you focus. You have to get strong and harvest your powers and be ready."

Ping flies away in the rain, leaving him with the resolution to harvest more power.

He gets up, grabs an empty bag that hangs from one of the dumpsters in the alley, and walks through town to grab birds to bring back to the alley to feed himself, building up his strength to fight Buru and save Purity, Abby, and this planet he stands on, Earth.

CHAPTER FIVE

A Clash in Time

Time moves on in Morgantown High as the school bell rings for lunch. Abby walks out the back door of the school, jostled around as everyone pushes their way through the small door. She beelines to the bleachers and sits down to read *The Magic of Time*. Running her fingers through the pages until she feels the space where the bookmark is, she opens the book to the title "Time Bender" and begins to read:

> *Section 15: The Power, Myth, and Creatures*
> *There is nothing more interesting than time itself. There is one powerful being that can manipulate such a thing but is unable to touch the future, and they're called "time benders." It's not like any science fiction movie where groups of people use a time machine to jump through time. Time benders are in control of time and can use their powers for good or evil. They can do two different types of time bending: 1) They can use their powers to relive time without disturbing it, or 2) Relive time to manipulate it for a different outcome. Time benders can also speed up or slow down specific areas and locations. Some people call them immortal, claiming they have learned to recycle their lifespan for thousands of years—*

The pages begin to move on their own, flipping violently, stopping on a different page and topic. On the top of the page is "Power Harvester," and she continues to read more.

Power harvesters are ones who can harness their powers and store them in safe keeping. They can store their power in other objects or even share their power with those objects. Myths state that people who can harness the power, or have an object that contains the power, can become as strong as the power harvesters themselves.

Abby's attention snaps to reality, as she can hear talking beneath her under the bleachers. This is where the "cool" kids usually hang out, doing the things they're not supposed to. Smoking, drinking, or simply cutting class go unpunished because behind the bleachers is a fence leading to the edge of school property, the hole hidden behind bushes. Someone like Abby would never be invited to a place like that nor did she want to ever be. Trying to be extra quiet, she listens closely.

"Can you believe I got detention for a week because she lost her cool?" Jennifer's voice is easily recognizable as she talks about their encounter from this morning and continues to rant, "She is not going to get away with this; I'm telling you this much."

"Just let it go, Jennifer. You're the one who is bothering her when she did nothing to you. She seems to be nice and bothers no one," Rachel says, catching her sister off guard.

"Are you going to take that, Jennifer?"

"Yeah, seems like your sister's choosing the wrong side here."

"Maybe she got dropped on the head too hard when she was younger," the groupies reply.

Jennifer walks up to Rachel and pushes her down to the ground. She falls on her heavy backpack with a loud thud, papers, candy, and bitten pencils spilling out as the girls begin to laugh and make fun of Rachel, calling her slow and an outcast. Jennifer snaps back at Rachel, "If you want, you can be her friend. If it wasn't for me being your sister, you would have been bullied just like her."

Abby listens closely and hears Rachel sniffling through her tears as the girls continue to taunt her. Her sadness turns into anger, and for the first time, she lashes out at her own sister, raising her voice back at Jennifer, "I bet I would because you'd be the one bullying me. Just because I'm different than the rest of you does not mean I deserve to be treated like this. I guess friends come first before family, right, Jennifer?" She gets up off the ground, shoving what she can back into her backpack and shuffling through the bleachers, holding her face as she runs back to school.

One of Jennifer's friends breaks the silence. "So, what do you have in mind for Abby?"

Jennifer pauses as she thinks. "I don't know right now, but when I do, she won't know what hit her." Abby stays very still as the chain fence rattles. The girls shuffle through the hole in the fence and off school property to cut school.

She closes the book, remaining quiet until she knows the coast is clear. As she sits there thinking about what she read, the books falling in the library and the pages flipping on their own, Abby realizes this has to be all Friend's doing, trying to see if she remembers him or something bigger. But why not just show her instead of all the hints?

From the reading, she discovered the reason why her necklace glows: Friend harvested his power into the crystal. That's why when Friend was hurt, he needed the necklace back to recharge his powers, leaving the question, "How did he run out?" Was it because of the mission? She tries to wrap her head around it all, but this does not explain the comet or the broken necklace he was holding when she first met him in her room. All she can do is think and search for clues, but she knows she's running out of time. Time until what, she doesn't know; she can just feel it.

The coast is clear as the bell rings for class to resume. Taking a deep breath as she looks at Morgantown High, it sinks in that she may be done with this school forever and have to leave Friend behind if he doesn't come back to her soon. She does not want to leave Morgantown without knowing more about him. With a sigh, she walks inside to finish up the rest of the school day.

The final bell rings with a flood of students pouring down the halls and out of the front door of the school. Abby is sucked into the wave of students, pushed and shoved and squeezed, riding the current outside. As the mass number of students dissipates, she feels a tap on her shoulder. She turns around and sees Rachel by herself, waving at her nervously.

"Hello, Abby, I, uhh…I just wanted to say hello and, well, umm…" An awkward pause stretches out as Rachel plays with her hands, looking lost in her own skin.

Abby breaks the awkwardness. "Is there anything else you want to say, Rachel?" She's unused to seeing Rachel without her sister.

"Well, yes, I mean, no, well…Yes, I do. You see, my sister is very angry at you, and well, she's planning to get back at you for putting her in detention. She said it was embarrassing, and I told her to get over it, and that didn't go well. She got even more mad and pushed me to the ground, so I just wanted to tell you to watch out because I don't know what she's planning. She won't tell me, and I don't want you to get hurt anymore."

Abby never had anything against Rachel and always knew she was being manipulated by her twin sister. She was always told what to do by Jennifer, and most of the time, Abby felt sorry for her for having to put up with all the name-calling from her own sister and her sister's friends. Because they've both been on the receiving end of Jennifer's bullying, she knows Rachel's concern is genuine. "Thanks for the heads-up, and I really mean it," Abby says, her sincerity shining through the big smile on her face.

Rachel replies back, "You're a really nice person. We may not know each other that well, but you're very nice to me, and I always liked your hair." As if to prove it, she leans in, gently tugging a strand of Abby's curly hair and letting it go so it bounces back. She then walks away in one direction, by herself for the first time, looking lost without Jennifer, as Abby goes the opposite direction, heading home to read more in the books.

She gets home and walks straight to her room. She locks the door behind her, anxious to read more. Throwing her backpack on her bed, she opens the older, weathered book, the one that opened in the library to page 115. Abby turns to that page with the title reading "The Unknown Tale of Harold Schweitzer and Amorosa."

Harold Schweitzer was an astronomer born in a small town in 1947, where he did his studies at home while caring for his ill wife, Amorosa, born with a rare and untreatable disease. While doing his research, he came across an uncharted area of exploration out in the darkness of the galaxies. He looked further to a planet that was quite large with many moons surrounding it. What made his discovery extraordinary and out of this world were the colors in that galaxy. What Harold Schweitzer found was a beam of bright blue light coming from the planet. Harold came to the conclusion it was a unique light source made by intelligent beings, and there was more out in the galaxy than just the people on Earth. Soon after his discovery, his wife passed away from her ailments, so he decided to name his discovered planet and galaxy after her.

Abby examines the picture of what Harold Schweitzer took from the lens of the telescope, a blue beam of light glowing in the dark depths of the galaxies, dead space in the background. She's quick to put one and one together; when Abby jumped onto the chatter, she remembers seeing a moon overlooking the beam of light the same color as the picture. This place called Amorosa is where Friend came from. That's why the book flipped to page 115; he wanted Abby to know. She continues reading.

> *With his discovery and thesis called* We're Not Alone, *he became very famous in a short period of time. Years passed, and with a mixture of fame, depression, and excitement, he became obsessed with his discovery, wanting to know more and how to get there, to the point where scholars, who were inspired by his discovery, became worried about his well-being. His discoveries became visions he claimed were faceless creatures from that planet, ranting to anyone who would listen. But just before he planned to announce his visions to the world on live television, he vanished with no proof of the faceless creatures, only his conviction driving him mad...*

As she reads deeper into the pages, the words begin to glow. She brushes her hand up against the page. *He discovered a planet with a blue light.* Abby looks up, suddenly noticing she is not in her room anymore but on someone's living room couch. She shuts the book as she finds her bearings.

The home is small with tall, rounded ceilings and artifacts and treasures neatly littered throughout, giving a rustic charm. A gust of wind comes from the stained glass window, brushing down her back.

The sound of her own voice rings from upstairs and sends a startling chill down her spine. "Friend, how are we going to get there without a portal?"

Friend growls in response, and her voice answers back, too low for Abby to hear.

Confused, Abby takes a stumbling step back, trying to keep silent as she wavers on the border of panic. Flapping wings descend the stairs. She searches for a place to hide, and when she turns around, she clamps a hand to her mouth so she does not scream as she is faced with Ping.

She feels tapping over her shoulder, making her jump, and as she turns, a yell rises in her throat, but a new hand covers her mouth. Abby blinks as she stares at herself but different, just like the little girl in the junkyard but older.

"Shh..." her other self says. "Let me, and only me, speak, and all I want you to do is nod. Do you understand?"

Abby nods yes.

"Do you know the names of the Nobles, the three Gods, or Buru?" Abby waves her hand in a so-so gesture, recognizing the name Buru from the chatter's timeline but not knowing his importance.

"Do you know Friend?"

She nods yes.

"Did he send you here?"

No, she shakes her head again.

The other Abby's eyes move erratically. "No, no, no, this can't be. You must be a sign of what's to come; this can't be an accident. I told him to teach me to fight more, but he won't now. He says we are ready enough. We can't speak here."

They vanish out of the house, reappearing by the shoreline. Abby looks up and notices how deep blue the sky is, some seagulls squawking while flying across the waves folding gracefully onto the shoreline. The sun is beaming on them as the warm air lightly blows the aroma of seaweed and salt water. As Abby turns around, she notices the house they were just in has a large telescope protruding from the second-floor window. Behind the house is a white, towering lighthouse that overlooks the large sea.

She drops her hand from Abby's mouth. "You can call me—"

Abby cuts her off. "Abigail…"

"How did you know that I was…? Did you meet me before? If we have met before, then does that mean, in my future, we crossed paths? Wait, don't tell me; you might change the future."

"So, you're Abigail." Abby shakes her head, hoping to jostle up some comprehension in her brain. "Let me get this straight. You are me, and I am you, and we are from different timelines? But if I was here before, then why don't I remember?"

"You don't remember this because you never lived in this timeline. For example, when you wake up in the morning, you have a routine, but what would happen when you change it? But it has to be drastic for it to work. That's why we look the same but with some differences."

"But you don't glow?"

"What do you mean?"

"In my timeline, you are in my necklace and talk to me in my dreams as a glow, saying this is not part of the plan."

"What plan?"

"Friend tried to show me events I didn't remember, and I still don't know why." Remembering the book still clutched in her hands, Abby lifts it now as she says, "I found a book in an old library about the discovery of his home planet, and while I was reading, it started to glow, and it brought me here."

"My question is, why am I in your necklace? I can only think of a couple reasons for that to happen. To keep me safe, not dead but hidden…I don't know." Abigail takes a step back, analyzing everything, her eyes growing wide with realization. "Did we lose?"

"Lose? What did you lose?"

Abigail agonizes some more, tapping her finger against her mouth as she walks past Abby to look out at the waves hitting the rocks. She appears scared when she says, "There has to be a good reason for me not to say anything to you. There has to be something that happens where, if I knew, it would change an outcome. I might have said too much. I don't want to change the future." Abigail nods, as if coming to a conclusion. "There is only one thing you have to do. Make sure Friend goes home."

Before Abby can let out a single word, Abigail's hand glows blue, still looking out at the ocean as she says to herself, "Everything will be okay." She blinks, shifting her gaze from the water to Abby, and places an open hand on her head. Abby watches tears run down Abigail's face, then everything turns white.

She comes to sitting on the bleachers, looking down at *The Magic of Time* in her lap. Voices mutter beneath her once more but, this time, talking about something different.

"Jennifer, can you believe it's going viral? Foster Trash has never been so popular." They laugh together with the audio from one girl's phone playing the sounds of water splashing and Abby's voice begging. The video of the toilet dunking treatment.

Abigail's voice comes forth. "Where did you go?!"

Abby whispers back, "I was reading the book in my room, then it started to glow, and the next thing I knew, I was in an old house with stained glass windows right next to a beach. You were there."

"What are you trying to say? You zoned out for twenty minutes with your eyes glowing blue."

"I went back in time, and you told me I clashed with time."

"Yeah, I can see that. You messed a lot up. Remember when those girls dragged you into the bathroom? Well, you were filmed, and they shared it to everyone. Do you also remember when you helped Friend in the woods, and he brought you back before that even occurred and you walked out of school?"

"Yeah?"

"Well, since you changed time, you never walked out of school."

"What about the library?"

"That happened because I brought you there, and those books stayed with you through the time jump. It's like leaving a footprint on time itself, like—"

"Only if it is significant enough. So, does that mean you are me, and that moment I saw you, or myself, happened and..."

"Well, well, well, look what we have here," the voice of Abby's nightmares sneers from beneath her. "I'm surprised I didn't smell you from a mile away."

Abby closes the book franticly, trying to put it back into her backpack.

"Hey, where do you think you're going? We're not done with you yet," Jennifer yells out.

Abby sprints down the bleachers as Jennifer and her groupies scramble to get out from underneath. She runs out onto the open field, Jennifer not too far behind. Abby heads toward the woods, knowing they won't follow her if she goes in, but she is running out of stamina. Jennifer reaches out to grab her backpack, but as soon as her fingers brush the fabric, Abby vanishes from thin air.

Abby appears in a foreign environment, an old building with unique architectural designs. The floor is white granite, the pillars and columns stone gray with sparkles of purple that glisten in the light. She turns around in front a very large, golden door, open but with no one around. She walks through and can hear the echoes of her footsteps bouncing off the walls, indicating how empty and vacant it really is. "Hello, is anyone there?" But no answer. She follows a carpet walkway, alive with swirls of red and gold, to the far end of the room. Steps lead up a platform with four large seats, more steps to a second platform holding three more large seats painted in gold. On either side are banners draped with an unfamiliar symbol, a diamond sitting atop a triangle with a red rectangle rising through the center of them and extending past the diamond. In the center of the room are different sizes of magnifying glasses with a red beam of light passing through each one, shooting up to the domed, pyramidal ceiling. Abby looks between the banner and the light mechanism, noting their similar shapes.

A portal opens, Ping flying through and catching her by surprise with the old man's voice coming from him. "Oh no, no, no, this is not good. Not even I can do such things. That you can means you may be even more powerful than Friend himself. But it's time to go back before much greater things happen." He perches on her shoulder.

"Ping, you can speak?"

"Speak, yes, but Ping, I am not," the old man's voice says, not coming from Ping this time but from behind her. She turns, seeing an old, withered creature with brown, wrinkly skin. His yellow, wide eyes sit on the far side of his head, and he's short in size, wearing a robe like a monk. Abby has no words to say, so he breaks the silence. "It's so nice to finally meet you in person, Abby."

"How do you know my—"

"We don't have much time to make small talk; I just want you to listen. This is Purity, where Friend is from. A dying planet on this side of the universe, seeking a new home, but we have lost so much in the process of searching."

The old creature gestures at the grand room before them. "Where you are standing is where the Nobles and Gods once stood hundreds of years ago. One day, the Gods were gone, so us Elders opened portals, searching for the Gods instead of a new home. So much time was wasted.

"The worlds we opened were too dangerous for us Elders, so the Nobles took our place in the search. We were so close to one of the three Gods, but for some reason, the portal closed, leaving the Nobles inside and the Elders waiting for their return. But with no Nobles and no Gods, we closed the doors. We wanted to keep the people hopeful, so we lied about the Nobles and Gods being gone, making them think they are still alive. But as time passed, our planet began to show signs of decay. Three hundred years later, I stand here, still waiting for their arrival while others lose hope or believe they were stories, but we Elders know the truth. The only way the planet stays alive is from the blue light from the glass."

Abby shoots a pointed look at the vibrant red beam. "But it's red?"

"When Friend left us, we lost a war we should have prevented. Friend was part of a group called the Five Purists, the ones sworn to protect, and they enforced the rules without using their powers, showing restraint. Always beating their chest, signifying protection to the people who live on this dying planet, and our people look up at a statue as a reminder of their greatness. Just like how you have a statue on your home planet."

"Who were you at war with?"

"One of the members of the Five Purists who used his powers and lost faith in Purity. He went rogue, coming back with an army of others who also lost their way. They should've all been stricken to the farthest moon."

"Stricken?"

"Yes, stricken; when one is from Purity, they have to abide by our laws, similar to Earth. When these laws are broken, a purest would need to be placed on a trial. If convicted, they would be stricken of their name and banished from Purity. They get sent to one of the four moons where they will survive on their own, stripped of their name as they are unworthy. Sadly enough, your Friend was also stricken before he left us."

Abby's jaw drops in shock. "What did he do?"

"He did nothing, and it was all my fault. As the Eldest Elder, I had to make tough decisions; I should have never let him fight. He was never a warrior; he is a protector, always sworn to protect.

I hope you understand he needs to come back home to take back what's left to start anew."

At the mention of starting anew, she looks around, a strange feeling building in her gut like a stone. The room is covered in dust. "Where is everyone who lives on this planet?"

The Eldest Elder's mood changes, flustered, as if he is hiding some key information. "Why ask such a silly question? Of course they are here. They are all here, alive and well. Us Elders take very good care of them, all of them. It has been difficult, but we have been managing."

She feels like he is hiding a lot in his story. "But you just said the planet is dying. That, to me, does not sound alive or well. And another thing," she adds as she remembers Ping perched on her shoulder, "why were you spying on me, disguising yourself as a bird?"

"With my powers, I can take control of the living, sense power in others, and create portals with the other Elders. I can sense true power in you, powers not even Friend knows of. I was this bird to stay connected and find a way to make a portal to bring him back. It's like finding a diamond in the galaxy—that's not easy to do." The Elder's gaze drifts up to the domed roof. "It is time for you to go. The portal will open soon in Court Square, just like last time. Tell him to be ready." The Elder moves his hand dramatically, as if doing a dance, and a portal opens up underneath her. Her heart lodges in her throat as she drops through, and her scream echoes back at her, deafening.

Abby falls for some time before she comes to, sitting up in her own bed and grabbing her chest. Tapping comes from her window; it's Ping. Outside, a bad storm rages with pouring rain. She runs over to the window, opening it for Ping to fly into her room and onto her bed, cleaning his feathers like normal.

"Thank you for waking me, Ping. I was in a bad dream, or was it…?" She's struck with an idea. "Okay, Ping, listen to me very carefully. I'm going to ask you some questions, and I want you to answer them, okay? When I ask you a question, I want you to peck at this book three times for yes and two times for no. Do you understand?"

Ping pays no mind to her request as she places one of her favorite books, titled *In A Dark, Dark Room* by Alvin Schwartz, next to him. He continues to clean himself.

"Okay, Ping, here is your question, and I know it might be silly. Are you a creature from a planet called Purity named the Eldest Elder who is going to open a portal to bring Friend back home to save the dying planet at war with Buru?"

Ping stops and looks at her with his head tilted off to the side, listening.

"Are you the Eldest Elder?"

He looks at the book, pecking his beak one, two, then three times. Her green eyes grow wide in shock.

Abigail's voice yells out, "Stop!"

Time comes to a sudden halt, stopping Ping from answering any more questions. He flies backward out the window as time goes into reverse, and the window slams shut, making Abby jump.

"Where have you been? One second, you were reading the book, then the timeline changed, then you ran into the woods and disappeared, then the whole day finished without you until you suddenly showed up here," says Abigail.

"Cece!"

"She doesn't know a thing. She was sitting inside the whole time. Time was stopped on her and no one else."

"Did you do it?"

"No, I couldn't have. That's not the point. You changed the timeline. This means there are voids in the timeline. This is not good!"

"I was looking into the book, and the words started to glow, and I was in an old house, and I saw myself there with your name,

Abigail, saying you were once me and telling me more about Friend and a portal and how time works, like how time can clash into each other. Then I came back, you were telling me how time changed, and I was spotted by Jennifer, so I ran into the woods, but when I did, I went to Friend's home planet, Purity. I met with the Eldest Elder, and he said the portal is coming to Court Square very soon and I have to tell Friend. Then he opened up a portal, and I fell through and woke up in my room. That is what happened." Abby gasps in a breath after that long-winded explanation.

"Wait, you said you saw yourself and called yourself Abigail. You think I'm you just because we share a name that sounds similar?"

"Yeah, we looked the same, but some things were different." Abigail chuckles.

"What's so funny?"

"When I said don't go searching for clues, what did you do? You went searching, and your mind starts wrapping itself into some interesting hypotheses. You don't understand anything, do you? That pretty, little necklace wrapped around your neck is linked to Friend."

"So?"

"So that means what you are seeing is his memories, but you saw yourself instead of who was really within his mind. Just like a dream."

"But I was interacting with myself," Abby protested. "And what about the Eldest Elder? He said he was inside of Ping, and when I asked him a question, he answered with my name. You're saying that's not real?"

"No, it is not real. Where you are right now is real, so stop thinking about Friend. He has a mission, and don't think of steering him off his path."

"A mission, like a portal opening for him to go home to his home planet. So you're telling me that is not real…? Why are you so quiet, Abigail? Is it because I am saying the truth about what this real mission is all about? You are the one who showed me the old library, and it was Friend who showed me where the books were. I think you are just like the Eldest Elder; you are hiding big portions of this story, and I'm going to get to the bottom of it, with or without you," Abby says with rage as her necklace glows.

Suddenly, night changes into day as she is unable to control her necklace's powers.

"I was the one who showed you where the books were. You're not the only one who has questions," Abigail says, sounding heartbroken.

Before Abby can say another word, her alarm goes off, and Cece's knocking on her door. "Girl, you better be up."

"I'm up, Cece, thank you." She sighs, tired from her mind running and trying to piece everything together and figure out where it all goes from here and losing trust with Abigail.

She gets ready for the new day, gathering her things for another afternoon at school. She makes her way to the dining room where something in the corner of her eye catches her attention. It's the envelope with the information of her potential parents. She can hear Abigail's voice echo through her head, "Stop thinking about Friend." She ignores Abigail's words, snatching the envelope and stuffing it into her backpack.

Her journey to school passes with no bizarre encounters or out-of-this-world time- stopping or jumping. Just a normal day. She walks to her locker to grab her books for class, no Jennifer or her groupies in sight. She blends in like a shadow in a crowd, a feeling she's always wanted.

Her classes for the first half of the day go by without any trouble as a normal freshman. The bell rings, and Abby walks through the halls as she thinks of the moments she's had down this very hallway where her locker rests. She tries to think of the good, but it quickly turns to negative as all she can think of is the bullying and torment she has gotten day after day right in front of her locker. It angers her as she reimagines herself being taunted, being shoved up against that same locker.

She sets her backpack down, reaching inside for the envelope she took from home this morning. Taking a seat on the nearest hallway bench, Abby opens it to find out about her new future. The little picture she saw before of the two potential parents falls out first, still giving her a warm, comfortable feeling. She turns the photo over, revealing more details on the two in the photo.

The woman's name is Julie Nolan, a freelance writer and artist. The man's name is Cole Nolan, a hard-working construction worker. There is another photo of a white house with dark gray trim and shutters with beautiful landscaping. They live out in the country, and she can see flat, clean land around the house, large plants along the pathway to the front entrance, and colorful sculptures, spiritic and interesting.

For the first time, she can see herself living in this home. Having space to run around and feel free and creative. She has that feeling of being wanted by Cole and Julie, and it's not forced. She remembers some of the homes she went to, and the photos they shared felt fake. With the professional photos and their perfect, fake smiles as they all wear matching clothes on their family trips, trying so hard to look fun, it always felt like she was being bribed to live their fake life, and that's not who she is.

But it's different with Julie and Cole; they seem real to her, not going all out with their photos, not showing an unrealistic life but instead, who they are. She feels eager to meet them, even though she still worries about Friend.

She flips through more documents, seeing they are high school sweethearts, recently married, and months apart in age.

A small pink envelope slips out from between two pieces of paper, dropping onto the floor by her feet. She scrambles to pick it up. The back of the envelope is held down with a glossy, gold sticker, raised up in the shape of a flower. She flips it over to the front with the words "Welcome to our home, Abby" written in a nice bubble font, each word in different colors. Slowly and carefully, she opens to a small letter inside, an explosive, colorful design of flowers around the border, with a written message that reads:

> *I know we haven't met yet, but it feels like I have known you for such a long time just by learning a little about you. We hope we are a perfect match for you. We want to grow together and go on many adventures, like gardening, and Cole will bring us fishing and so much more. We can't wait to see you, Abby.*
>
> *- From Julie and Cole*

Reality sets in. She's overcome with cold feet as she's pulled in separate directions, having to choose between Friend and a new life in a new home with a new family. Her breathing quickens into short, shallow bursts as she has mixed emotions, not knowing whether to be sad or excited. With no sense of which direction to choose, she can only think of one person to talk to. She runs down the hallway, makes a sharp left, continues on, and makes another sharp turn, right to a door. She rushes through into an office.

She stares in panic as an office employee stands up out of her chair, yelling out, "You can't just barge in here. Come back here and fill out this check-in form."

Abby pays no mind to her demands as she makes her way through the office and down the hall to the last door. She whips open the door, catching Ms. Perez by surprise.

"Oh, Abby, I was not expecting you today...What's wrong?"

Abby can see the worry in her eyes as she stands with her arms tight to her chest, the letter clenched between her fingers. She doesn't know where to begin to say how she feels.

Before she can utter a single word, Ms. Perez's eyes drop to the envelope in her hands and is quick to put all the pieces together. "Come sit. I am so happy you came." She adjusts the papers on her desk, subtly pushing a box of tissues forward. "So I see you were reading about Julie and Cole. What did you find?"

Abby sits, taking a deep breath. "I found a lot, and they seem happy to meet me. I feel different about them, different than the other families, in a good way. But I don't think I'm ready to leave."

Ms. Perez leans forward. "Then when will it be the right time? If you feel so good about this opportunity, then what's holding you back?"

Abby knows Friend and the mysteries that lie with him are keeping her in Morgantown. "I feel weird that people, who I never met, want to know me and want me to be a part of their life. People who want to become parents to a stranger when I never knew where I came from or who my parents really were."

"Maybe this is a sign for you. Everything you read in that envelope seems to be perfect, but you're fighting yourself to stay here. What good did this town do for you?" Ms. Perez's face morphs into a sympathetic smile. "What I'm trying to say is I know you've been bullied here. Teachers have reported finding you crying in the hallways and the library, and I would always get the green slip of paper."

She opens her filing cabinet, pulling out a folder with a short stack of green papers inside. "Abby, this is your folder of all the times teachers have reached out to me, worried about you, your home, and school life. Unfortunately, they never had any proof, so I couldn't suspend who I suspected to be bullying you without their parents throwing a fit and having me fired. But see, in your folder on the top is the last incident. It reads here you finally stood up for yourself but got dragged by the hair and had your face dunked into the toilet. How we know this is because it became viral almost instantly, and we had the evidence needed to expel Jennifer and suspend the others involved. They won't return until you leave Morgantown, for good this time, because these people who chose you are the right match. Don't fight to stay here."

Abby exhales a shaky, relieved sigh. Jennifer is gone. Finally. "But what if it's too good to be true?"

"And what if it's not?" Ms. Perez tilts her head thoughtfully. "Starting today, forget what's gone, appreciate what remains, and look forward to what's coming. You can always visit Morgantown, but it's time for you to start fresh. This is just a chapter of your life closing with many more chapters to open." She gives Abby a confident grin.

Abby smiles back, taking in a deep breath. "Maybe you're right. My heart is not made for Morgantown. I think you convinced me to move on, and I feel excited to meet my new family. Thanks for making the time to talk to me so suddenly."

"You're very welcome, Abby, and don't hesitate to come back here if you need someone to talk to."

"Okay, thanks again." She grabs her backpack, swinging it over her shoulder with confidence, and heads back to class.

"Oh, Abby, I forgot to remind you about our agreement."

Abby stops in her tracks. "Our agreement?"

"The fall social is today, and remember, you promised me to give it a shot. I know Morgantown is not the right match for you, but I think it's best, since your bullies are gone from the school, to participate in the social. I think it would give you at least one good memory of this place before you go."

In Abby's mind, she is screaming, "No," but she must play off her emotions for now. "I didn't forget, Ms. Perez. I'll be there, I promise."

"A promise is a promise." Ms. Perez smiles back, happy with Abby's decision.

Abby turns away with a straight face, annoyed that she feels forced to be involved in social activities.

She sits at her desk, still feeling like a shadow, like she doesn't have to look over her shoulder. The class is quiet with the classroom light off as they watch an educational video projecting onto the whiteboard. Abby splits her focus between the video and making sketches of Friend inside her notebook. She wants to move on but can't stop thinking about him.

A blue glow shines onto her notebook, catching her off guard. It is her necklace, shining bright. She grabs the crystal as an overwhelming pain strikes in her head. She drops her forehead to her desk to hide the pain as Abigail's voice emerges, catching her by surprise. "Where is Friend?!" she yells.

Abby glances around, but everyone's zoned out and not paying attention. Angling herself toward the window, she says under her breath, "I don't know what you're talking about. I thought you knew where he was. You told me not to worry about him."

"You need to leave. You messed up too much time."

Abby, with great frustration, grabs her belongings and marches out of the classroom's back exit, still holding tight to her necklace. Nobody notices her leave. As soon as she closes the door behind her, she snaps at Abigail, "Maybe he went through the portal and completed the mission, like you always wanted."

"It's not what I want; it's what needs to happen."

Abby rolls her eyes. "I need to get back to class."

"But I need your help."

"You told me to move on! I'm listening to you." She winces as her raised tone sounds magnified in the empty hallway. "You also said Friend needs to go home, sounding so callous and cold. For someone claiming to care for him, you want him to leave so badly. Now you come to me in desperation. I thought you knew where he is?"

"That's true, but—"

"It's time for me to move forward in my life! Figure it out yourself."

"You clashed through time! Changing significant time events. And when Friend brought you back from the junkyard house, he never left with you. I can feel him and his powers, but he feels far away. This has happened before, but that was when the portal opened. I am afraid. Because of the time jumps, the worst is bound to repeat itself."

Abby stops to take a second to think and let Abigail's words sink in. "Fire and ash."

"Yes, and that's what I'm afraid of now."

"Before I help, all those visions and memories with Friend, were they true?"

"I think he was trapped in the junkyard timeline. The memories and events that once happened."

"From the junkyard?"

"Yes, and it's much more than that. I got it! When you left to go back into the timeline from the book, accidentally you must have triggered the clash in this timeline. That must have helped him come back to this timeline since you are both connected, using the powers in different wavelengths."

"Is that why some of the events that happened were changed back?"

"Exactly! Events that Friend has changed has reverted back as if he was never here, like the video."

"Sounds believable, but are you sure? Why did it take so long?"

"I'm most certainly positive. Even time itself needs a little time for things to work."

"So, now what?"

"I would like to share the truth, but I still can't afford the mission to fail. When this is all over and the portal is opened, I'll show you everything you want to know, but for now, we need to find out where Friend is. What do you say? Do you want to help me out?"

Abby hesitates, debating whether to trust Abigail to finally share the truth. "Okay, I will help you. Only because I don't want fire and ash to happen to Morgantown. I want you to also keep your promise to tell me everything I don't know, to fill in all the missing pieces."

"Deal, but we have to act fast. He's close, and the portal is going to open soon. I can feel it."

"I agree, but I have to stay in school. I can't skip. The less eyes on me, the better. Trust me."

"Okay, I trust you. I'll try to figure out some clues while I wait." Abigail leaves with the necklace dimming back to normal.

Abby sighs, saying to herself, "Friend, where are you now? What are your plans?" With no one to respond back, she turns around and heads back into class.

Students eager to attend the fall social begin to rush out of their classrooms to the sound of the bell ringing. Abby travels down the traffic-crammed hallway. Scattered freshmen, sophomores, juniors, and seniors shove their way through the gymnasium doors. Teachers shout at students to slow down, pointing out and reprimanding some by name, while trying to manage a safe entrance. Abby turns away and leans on the nearby lockers, waiting for the entryway to clear up before entering.

She finally enters the gymnasium where the handmade banner reads, "Fall School Social," with a paper mâché, bare tree in the center, followed by dwindling leaves and hand-turkey drawings. Abby stands close to the exit, as she does not know what to expect. The gymnasium holds a full-size basketball court with bleachers sitting students on either side. A scoreboard hangs over the center court. There is a wall banner covered with jersey numbers matching the mascot colors of the school, red and black with the logo of a knight holding a shield and sword, "Morgantown Knights" printed on the bottom.

The large quantity of students at the social begins to give her anxiety, and she feels uncomfortable, her body tensing up. Abby throws her hoodie over her head, trying to disguise herself.

A student walks to Abby and hands her a flyer. "Here, take one," the student says before turning around and walking toward a group of students, handing out more flyers.

Abby reads the flyer and realizes there are a list of games and activities that will be held at the social. The gymnasium has stations filled with props, such as artificial, colorful leaves, pumpkin cutouts, and red, green, and blue streamers. On one side of the court, she observes more activities, such as a pumpkin carving station and a caramel apple dunking area.

Abby begins to plan her escape, overwhelmed with the number of students in one place, wondering which ones watched the video. She turns to exit the gymnasium when Mr. Booker approaches her. "Hello there, Abby, how are you enjoying the social?"

"Good, I guess," she says apathetically.

"I understand this is a huge transition for you, but I promise, you will have a great time." Abby looks up at Mr. Booker, giving him a slight grin.

"Okay, I'll try."

"Listen, Abby, I understand this may seem intimidating, but you must overcome these fears. I heard from Ms. Perez you have a special meeting coming up soon. I hope it goes well," Mr. Booker says as Abby notices he is wearing a green sweatband on his wrist and upper arm.

Ms. Perez stands in the center of the gymnasium, holding a microphone. "May I please have everyone's attention?" The students begin to settle down and listen in to Ms. Perez speak. "Welcome to our annual fall school social. For those who may be experiencing our fall social for the first time, I would like to welcome you in joining us in this event. This is a great opportunity to meet your peers, as we want everyone to come together and have a great time with all the games and activities we have planned for today.

"Teachers who are wearing colored sweatbands, please refer to your sign-up sheet to gather your red, green, or blue team color t-shirts and have your team stand in a line. The three games that will be held in the social today are egg on the spoon, a Hula-Hoop spin-off, and potato sack race. All points will be collected by the end of the games, and the winning team will receive a pizza bash."

Ms. Perez begins to read the names aloud for each team, starting with red, blue, and finally green. When Ms. Perez finishes reading the last couple of names, she notices Abby's name is not on the list. "Abby, are you on a team?" Ms. Perez says, her voice carrying across the crowded gym to where Abby still lingers by the exit.

"Umm…I didn't register to be a part of a team," Abby says.

"No worries, we will find a team for you."

Mr. Booker overhears the conversation and walks up to Abby. "Would you like to join the green team? I think you'll be great, and you can meet some of your peers," he offers enthusiastically.

"I don't know…Sports aren't one of my strong suits, and I'm not too competitive," Abby responds in an unsure tone.

"There is nothing better than playing a competitive sport with your team. It teaches good sportsmanship."

"I need everyone to get into their teams!" Ms. Perez says as she explains the rules for the first game over the microphone.

"I guess I'll join the green team."

"Great, here is your t-shirt!" Mr. Booker says to Abby with a big smile on his face, waving the other teammates to congregate by the bleachers.

While Abby glances at her team, she promptly realizes some of the students on her team were bystanders to her bullying and humiliation by Jennifer and her posse. She feels insecure in her decision to work with her fellow peers because she has no friends in school, and she's afraid they will judge her. Mr. Booker and the team head toward the other teams near Ms. Perez.

"Okay, everyone, the first game will be egg on the spoon. Choose your teammate wisely, as balance is the key factor to this game. It's quite simple and self-explanatory: an egg is placed on the spoon, you have to walk from one side to midcourt, and hand off the spoon with the egg to the other player who has to then walk from midcourt to the other side. It sounds simple, but it's much harder than you think."

Abby joins her team in a huddle as they discuss who will participate in the game. They collectively choose the two students. Abby stands aside and sits on the bleachers with her other teammates while waiting for the game to start.

After Mr. Booker speaks to the participants, he walks over to Abby. "You'll get your turn soon." Abby looks up with a disinterested smile.

The contenders get into positions as Ms. Perez starts counting down. "Three, two, one, go!" Screaming and yelling erupt, and cheers roar as the first round of students pace themselves, trying not to drop the egg. Abby watches on but does not cheer on her team. The first students gently hand the spoon and egg to the second students. "Go, go, go!" is heard all over the gymnasium as the second students in the green and red teams pass the finish line in a tie.

"Okay, everyone, great job!" She posts the team scores on a portable dry-erase board.

The red and green team scored ten points while the blue team scored zero. The contestants walk toward the bleachers to join their teams. As the two students approach, Mr. Booker reaches up to give them high fives. "Great job out there!" The other teammates praise them for winning the game.

"Students, please line up by the Hula-Hoop stations," Ms. Perez says.

"Okay, who wants to participate in this game?" Mr. Booker says hastily while other teams have their students standing by the Hula-Hoops. Some of the students start to argue why they would be best for the challenge, bypassing Abby as an option once more. Mr. Booker chooses two students to partake in the Hula-Hoop match.

Ms. Perez explains the students from each team will Hula-Hoop against an opposing team member for one minute and thirty seconds. While the music is playing, the student has to maintain a Hula-Hoop on their waist, and if it doesn't fall, they win points for their team.

The music starts, and each teammate works hard to keep the Hula-Hoop on their waist, swaying side to side. Some fail to keep the toy moving. When time is up, Ms. Perez stops the music. The total points are displayed on the dry-erase board again; the red and green teams earn thirty points each as the blue team earns fifteen points.

"Two teams are tied. This is going to be interesting with our last and final game, potato sack racing!" Ms. Perez waves her arms, eliciting excited cheers from the crowd. "Now, each team is only allowed to pick four participants, and the same rules as the egg on the spoon race apply. Teams will start off on one end of the court. Each player will hop around a cone and tag their teammate next in line. Then the next person in line gets into the sack and hops around the cone course. The team to finish first will have the chance to win double their team's total points," Ms. Perez explains as the students deicide once more who will compete in the race.

Mr. Booker nominates Abby, along with students who have not played so far.

"Are you sure? We could lose," a student asks Mr. Booker.

A senior also disagrees with the suggestion, and another teenager nods their head to the objection.

Abby agrees with the team. "I don't think that's a good idea. I don't want to mess it up for the rest of the team. A lot is at stake."

"You're part of the team, and I'm saving the best for last," Mr. Booker responds despite tension among the team.

"Okay..." Abby says as she walks toward Ms. Perez handing out the burlap sacks.

"Abby, it is so great to see you participating and socializing," she says, handing Abby the sack.

"Yeah, thanks." Abby takes the sack and lines up with her other teammates. Her palms start to sweat, and she waits to put her legs into the sack.

"Okay, everyone, ready, set, go!" Roars rage instantaneously, and the teams cheer as the race begins. The jumping shakes the ground beneath Abby's feet as she stands behind her teammates, leaving her to race last. Abby's legs shake within the burlap sack as she reaches out her hand to be tagged into the race. As she starts hopping, she hears cheers from Mr. Booker and her teammates.

"You can do it, Abby!"

"Let's go, green team, let's go," followed by stomping in between.

Abby gains confidence for the first time in her life. She is so close to the finish line. Abby feels a sense of togetherness as her team helps her trudge through her shyness; she powers through her exertion. Concentrating on her jumps, she looks up, which is a mistake. The sight of what awaits her on the other side of the finish line makes her stumble, losing distance between her and her competitors.

She sees herself at seven years of age, glowing blue, waving herself on. "Come on, you can do it," her younger self cheers with a boost of assurance. Abby's hops become larger in an already tight race, inching her way to first place, and her younger self vanishes as she barrels past the finish line.

"Green team wins!" Ms. Perez cries out, and Abby's team races to her side.

She wears a big smile on her face, yelling, "I did it, I did it!" As her team hugs her wholeheartedly, she feels warm inside. Abby has always desired that interaction and embrace.

The bell rings for lunch, and Ms. Perez makes a final announcement. "Okay, everyone, please return to your classes as we get the prizes for first, second, and third places. Have a great rest of your day! Great job, everyone." Students rush out of the gymnasium and flood into the lunchroom, as there are extra desserts and lunches set for the students.

Students from other teams congratulate Abby. "Good game, freshman," one of the seniors tells Abby. Others show good sportsmanship before exiting the gymnasium.

Abby's bright smile grows larger on her face. "Thanks," she replies, too late as he is too far to hear her. She grips herself tight, anxious from all of the positive attention she is receiving, making her feel overwhelmed with emotion.

"Abby, I am so happy to see you kept your word, participating in the events." Abby turns around. Ms. Perez walks over to her, smiling and dabbing the sweat off her forehead.

Abby is still trying to catch her breath. "A promise is a promise," Abby replies, adrenaline still coursing through her.

"You are right about that. You see how, sometimes, if you try different activities that are out of your comfort zone, it can really show you a different perspective. I'm glad you've created some good memories here before you go."

"Yeah, you were right after all. I gained some confidence out there. I felt very included and accepted by my classmates."

"Good! I'm so happy to hear that, Abby. Now, I have to prepare for a meeting, so I'll be seeing you at the conference with your potential parents in the next couple of days. Remember, keep an open mind," Ms. Perez reminds Abby.

Abby slightly grins, nodding, feeling an immense pressure to impress her new family, but at the same time, she wants Abigail to help her find closure with Friend before leaving Morgantown for good.

CHAPTER SIX

Can't Let Go

With school over, Abby rushes home, making her way up the stairs into her bedroom. She locks the door as she races to her bed, throwing her backpack on the floor, and her necklace glows as Abigail begins to speak, "I don't know where he can be. I can feel him and his powers, but it feels like he's far away, as if he's hiding."

"Hiding? What would he be hiding from?"

"I don't know, but something is wrong. He would never shut himself out like that."

Abby pauses. "Didn't you tell me he had a plan? Maybe this is part of his plan."

"No, something happened, but I can't put my finger on it. It all changed when he was showing you events to see if you remembered."

"So, you're saying since we last saw him, everything changed. Do you think it was because of the timelines clashing into each other?"

"No, it can't be...Wait, you might be onto something here. We went back in time, and he left us while he was still at Isabelle's house."

"Who's house?"

"At the junkyard. There is no time to explain why I know that right now, but what I'm thinking is since he was in the past and we went into the past on two time lengths, it messed up the sequence."

Abby puts her hands on her head. "This is all confusing."

"Confusing but plausible."

"When I was in the library, Mrs. Baker...she knew who I was. Do you think I changed the timeline?" Abby pulls one of the library books from her backpack and opens to a random page. She turns to another and another, but every word on every page is covered in a black ink where the words cannot be read. "No, no, no..." Abby says to herself. She flips through the pages, frantically searching for a clear page to read. Once she's about to give up, she stumbles across the last page. It is marked up with writing: "Some of us remember." Mrs. Baker said those exact words. Abby slams the book shut, her heart racing. She needs to go back to the old Morgantown Library for her next clue.

Abby swings open her door and runs down the hallway, flying downstairs as fast as she can. She reaches the front door, hand on the doorknob, when the voice of Cece behind her snaps, "Where do you think you're going?"

She quickly turns, her hand still on the doorknob. "I was going to go back to the library to give back these books."

Cece gives Abby a stern glance. "Okay. Did someone speak to you today at school?"

"Yes, my guidance counselor, Ms. Perez."

"Did she explain to you how important it is for you to be on time and not to hide during the meet and greet?"

"Yes, I'll make sure I'm here on time. I promised her I would—"

"Sixteen," Cece says with a strained sigh. "That is how many potential homes you had. Don't let this be number seventeen. As you get older, girl, less people want you, so don't mess this up, do you understand?"

"I understand."

"We'll see about that. A promise is a promise until the day comes, and that's tomorrow."

Abby's eyes grow wide in shock. "But Ms. Perez told me—"

Cece is quick to lose her patience, cutting Abby off, "I don't care what that woman told you. I'm telling you this: you have until tomorrow. They will be here in the afternoon to meet with you for the very first time, and that's it, that simple. You got that?"

"Yes," Abby says, trying to keep it short to please Cece.

"Go before it gets dark. Don't make the same mistake you did last time."

"I won't, I promise."

Cece motions with her head, dismissing her. Abby spins around, trying not to waste any more time as she hurries to the other side of town.

She runs as fast as she can with an armload of heavy books, struggling to hold on, but when she makes it to the Morgantown Library, the books slip from her slack fingers. "No, how is this possible?!" Abby says aloud. An empty lot stretches before her with tall, wild grass but no library, as if it was never there. All that remains is a "For Sale" sign that looks like it's been up for some time now. "Abigail, I need to go in there. Change it back," she says but with no answer. Abby groans with frustration as her clues lead into a dead end.

A man stops a few feet away, waiting to cross the street. She gathers up her books and quickly walks up to him. "Excuse me, sir, I have these books to bring back to the library, but it's gone. Do you know what happened to the library?"

The man sighs as he looks down at her, visibly not in the mood to speak. "What does that have to do with me?" he responds, while looking both ways for oncoming traffic. Abby still standing by his side, irritates the man. "This place hasn't been open for the last seven years and was taken down the week it closed, so you're a bit late. If I were you, I would just keep the books, kid. Does that answer satisfy you?"

"I have one more."

"Listen, I have to go." He says, while starting to cross the busy street. Abby walks a quarter away from the sidewalk into the street to hear his response.

"There was an old lady who worked here, Mrs. Baker. What happened to her?"

"I don't know much about her, okay? All I know is that old bat lost her mind and snapped. Her family put her in a home and is selling the land." Before she can say anything else, the man walks across the street, not caring about her or her questions.

Maybe Mrs. Baker knew more than people think, just like the homeless man in Court Square. There may be more to the story that Friend is trying to bring to her attention. Perhaps there's even more to Friend's story. How did the homeless man know how Friend sounds and how Morgantown is leveled with fire and ash? Or why was Mrs. Baker hesitant to give Abby the book? Why are parts of the book crossed out and written on?

Abby takes a long pause from her deep thinking, trying to put any pieces together instead of discovering more questions, but unfortunately, she has reached a dead end. Mrs. Baker is not there, and she has no idea where the mysterious homeless man is. She looks down at her necklace. "Come on, show me a sign. I'm running out of time." When nothing happens, Abby turns to head back home, disappointed and feeling empty inside.

The sun sets on another day and still no sign of Friend. She walks home, sad, defeated, and exhausted with only one day to go until she has to say goodbye to Morgantown and Friend as a whole. Abby thinks back on how Friend came into her life, wounded and battered, needing Abby's help. For the brief time she has known him, he's been nothing but a friend to Abby, more than she's ever had with anyone in her school or Morgantown. She waits until she's home, bedroom door shut, before crying as she thinks about Friend and how she was unable to help him.

With her face buried into her pillow, Abigail says to her, "Abby, I can't tell you everything. It's difficult to understand."

"Abigail, a part of me feels like I have known him for a long time, but I haven't. Then there's another part of me...I don't know, I have this feeling the clues aren't helping. I'm forced to remember moments so unforgettable, but even those moments I can't remember. And these clues, all of them, always lead to a dead end as if they don't want to be answered."

"What are you trying to say, Abby?"

"I think you know what I'm saying. You don't want me to know anything and never did. Ever since Friend came to me and you showed me the library, you wanted to block every step he took without him knowing you're alive. Just like you said, this was not a part of the plan. You wanted me to run around in circles. What are you hiding?"

Abigail makes a surprised, choking sound, the accusation is a punch to the throat. "If only you knew the type of mission this is. All of this—"

"What? All you talk about is this mission. What if he already changed the timeline and the worst is not going to happen?"

"Oh, right, Abby, it's that simple. Just because you figured out my plan, now you think you know everything."

"No, I am not saying that—"

"Here's a question since you think you know Friend so well: where is he?" Abby's unable to answer the question. "Here is one that has been under your nose the whole time: your little bird friend."

"Ping?"

"Ping, right! I remember telling you I would have chosen a different name, like stalker. That bird is something much greater, spying on your every move because they need Friend more than we do. Listen, I am sorry for misleading you; it's just important for him to go home."

"So the Eldest Elder was real this whole time, and what he is saying is true?" Abby isn't mad at Abigail, just disappointed she was purposely misled. "Abigail, I have one question; if you were with him the whole time, then why does he not show me you, or why don't I remember you?" Abby gets no response.

Knocking comes from the other side of Abby's door. She lifts her head, shouts, "Go away," and drops her face back into the pillow.

Her door swings open with Cece on the other side, a bag in her hand. "Get up, girl, get up. You're running out of time. You need to get your things together. Come on, girl, get up. You need to pack your things." Cece nudges Abby in the back, but she buries her face further into her pillow, not planning on moving. Cece drops the bag beside the bed. "This room better be all situated by the end of the day tomorrow," she says coldheartedly as she leaves.

When the door closes, Abby releases all of her feelings, sobbing into her pillow and crying herself to sleep, upset about leaving without saying goodbye to Friend.

She wakes up to her last day in Morgantown. It's a weird feeling as she gets up, sluggish and depressed, knowing today is it. She gets ready for her final day, and before leaving, Cece stops her once again at the front door. "Don't be late. They will be here around dinnertime."

She gives a soft nod with no words to describe how upset she really is about leaving without knowing more about Friend. She leaves, walking to school for the final time. While everyone else takes their normal routes, she knows this is her last. In a last-ditch effort, she takes a shortcut through Court Square to see if the homeless man is there, but no luck. Neither him nor Ping are there, making her feel more alone as she walks to Morgantown High.

Arriving at school on time like usual, today seems a little different. She notices the more popular students huddled together. As Abby walks past them, some of the girls dart an evil stare at her, while still doing nothing. Abby knows that their staring because of the video, resulting in Jennifer being expelled and her friends being suspended.

She walks to her locker and sees Rachel by herself, looking lost and confused as she stands alone, holding her loose, crumpled papers and textbooks in her hands. Her grip slips, and all her papers litter the floor as kids laugh at her. She scrambles to pick them up, repeating to herself, "I'm sorry, I'm sorry, I'm sorry." Rachel is defenseless without her sister around.

Jennifer's groupies walk up behind Rachel. "Watch where you're going, Fisheyes," one of the girls yells out at Rachel before bumping into her, her papers flying out of her hands once again.

With all them laughing, Rachel gets flustered, still apologizing for something she didn't do. "I'm sorry, I'm sorry, I'm sorry."

All Abby can do is spectate, not wanting to interfere and become the next target. "So, do you think you have full protection even when your sister's not here? Well, think again," one of the girls says before walking away with the rest of the group, leaving Rachel with an expression of loneliness.

Abby shuts her locker, giving Rachel a final look. They lock eyes, and she gives Rachel a little wave before walking to her first class for the last time.

Time moves on to fourth period, study hall, where Abby usually sits in the back of the classroom, distant from the rest of the class so she can get most of her homework and classwork done. She is happy no one knows today is her final day. The less spotlight on herself, the better. Instead of working though, she opens the other old book from the old Morgantown Library as discreetly as she can.

In the corner of her eye, a chair pulls out beside her. Rachel sits down, catching her off guard as she tries to hide the book. "Hey, Abby...Is it okay if I sit here?"

"Uhh…okay, sure?" Abby discreetly slides the book under the table onto her lap.

"I'm sorry if this is awkward for you. I just…I don't know where to sit since my sister isn't here."

Abby plays sympathetic, as if she really cares to know where her bully is. Knowing Rachel will say anything, Abby doesn't hesitate to ask, "So where is she?"

Rachel sighs. "They posted a video of your head being dunked in the toilet, and they deleted it, but Ms. Perez and the principal found out, and they said she might not be allowed back. My parents are really mad at her." Abby is so happy her final day in Morgantown High is with Jennifer nowhere in sight. Rachel smirks and continues, "I guess you're happy she's not here, right, Abby?" Abby laughs alongside Rachel, bonding together and, for the first time ever, feeling comfortable inside the classroom.

From the corner of Abby's eyes, she sees Jennifer's groupies pointing and rolling their eyes at Rachel, trying to listen in. "Hey, don't listen to them. They're just nosy," she says to Rachel.

"Yeah. They're just mad I told on them for skipping school and posting the video. They're always mean to me because I'm not like my sister. You know, I'm just different."

Rachel's gaze dips, and she changes the topic. "What's that book you have there?" Abby's heart sinks, caught with the book she's been trying to keep a secret. She shows Rachel, who reads the title aloud, "*The Unknown Universe*. Wow, that's an old book, Abby. Where did you get it? It looks like it belongs in the old Morgantown Library."

"The library? Why would you think that?"

"Oh, you didn't know? My grandmother owned the Morgantown Library. Before she lost her mind, of course. We put her into an old folk's home, but she didn't last long. She passed away soon after. I used to help her all the time putting books away."

This is a major breakthrough in her search for clues, and knowing Rachel, she'll tell Abby everything she knows. "How did she lose her mind?"

"From what I remember, seven years ago, she went to the doctor with my mom and dad, and they told us she had early signs of dementia, but every single time she spoke, she knew what she was talking about. She always told me there is more to the story, and no one wants to hear her because no one remembered—"

"What story?"

"She said a girl came through a portal with a creature with no face who wore a suit, and she said they were fighting another monster together. She would always say no one stayed in the circle, and that's why no one remembers."

Abby's heart skips. "Was the circle a blue dome?"

"Yeah! That's what she called it, the dome! How did you know?"

"Uhh…I had a hunch," she lies, and thankfully, Rachel believes her. "Did she say anything else?"

"Not really. One day, she was just different, and we didn't understand her anymore. Oh!" Rachel exclaims, eyes alight with a memory. "There was just one other thing she said. She told us the girl came back and her monster is coming back, and that's when she lost her mind. Her whole library looked like a tornado blew through it the day she lost it. I'm confused how you got this book to begin with. Can I see it?" Now it makes sense why Mrs. Baker was so concerned about Abby taking the books, and when Abby went into the past and fought the chatter, those events happened, but Mrs. Baker didn't remember. Rachel's parents used that event to close down the library.

She hesitates to let Rachel see the book, but maybe she's on to something, so she slides the book over. Rachel flips over the back of the hardcover to look behind it where Mrs. Baker stamped the slip card.

"Oh, that's interesting. It says here whoever last took the book was around the time when...well, that's when we brought her to the home, and the library closed. That's when her story changed to 'she's back.' We never knew or understood who she was talking about, but she would always say, 'She's the one who stole my books.'"

"But that was seven years ago, right?" Abby is in shock, realizing she changed time on her own to retrieve these books. All she can think is maybe Friend made people forget but let some remember for the clues to be answered.

"Who did you get this book from?"

"I found it in donations in the school library," Abby lies and quickly steers the topic back to her grandmother. "I have one more question to ask you about your grandmother. Do you know anyone else who saw the things she did? From what I know, no one else knew about a portal, the dome, or a monster." Her necklace vibrates with energy, and she grabs it tight so Rachel or anyone else can't see it.

Rachel gives her a strange look. "Is everything okay, Abby? I'm sorry if I scared you."

"No, Rachel, I'm fine. It's just that I...I have to go get some books from my locker."

The deflection catches Rachel off guard. "Uhh...okay...?"

"Thank you so much for telling me about your grandmother and her experiences. You have no idea how much that means to me," Abby says to a confused Rachel.

Abby gets up from her desk as she gathers her things, walking out of the classroom in a panic. She walks as fast as she can to the nearest bathroom and swings open the door to the nearest stall, locking it with shaky fingers. She releases her hand from her necklace, but there's nothing, not even a dim light, just another false alarm. Annoyed, she kicks the stall door as she feels more pressure that time is running out. "Why can't I help you?" she says to herself.

Before she can get out, the bathroom door swings open with Jennifer's groupies talking as they enter. She stays perfectly still with her legs up on the stall door, making sure they cannot see or hear her.

"Can you believe Rachel went behind her own sister's back and ratted her out and is now BFFs with Foster Trash?"

"Yeah, I know, that slow idiot is too stupid to keep her mouth shut."

"She thinks we'll have her back just because she's Jennifer's sister, but she has another thing coming. I'm sorry, but she's just too weird to look at." They all laugh as they leave the bathroom, the sound of the bathroom door swinging open, then closed.

Abby sympathizes with Rachel for what she has to put up with every day, and she knows how that feels. Maybe those girls don't know what a friend really is or understand how to treat other people.

She walks out of the bathroom to go back to her class, and as she turns the corner, she freezes. The men in the suits, the ones who were with Ms. Perez, are standing in front of her classroom. She hides behind the corner, pressing her body up against the lockers so they don't see her. They're here to make sure she makes it to the meeting with the new family on time, but she's not ready. She's come so close to Friend. She just needs a little more time. Considering where to go next with her clues, she knows she can't stay at school. The men would stop her. She needs to go back home to gather her things and leave on her own to figure out more.

She runs through the halls, skipping school with no intent to turn back. She races home, running up the brownstone stairs, swift and quiet as she makes her way to her room. Picking up the bag Cece left by her bed, Abby opens all her drawers and stuffs her clothes inside, grabbing books, pencils, and anything she can find, not planning to come back. She swings her bag over her shoulder and wastes no time escaping down the hall.

A voice speaks behind her, "Leaving so soon?" It's Cece, waiting at the other end of the hall, looking annoyed and disappointed at Abby.

"Cece, it's not what it…Let me explain. There is—"

"There is a lot to explain. You skipped school, and it looks like you're packing your things to leave early."

"Cece, I don't have time. I have to—"

"Listen, girl, this is your last opportunity, and I'll tell you this much: this is your last stay with me. Don't do anything you'll regret."

Abby bristles at the threat. Throughout all the years, Cece has been nothing but coldhearted. She just needs a little more time, but she's constantly being hit with roadblocks. "Cece, please don't threaten me. I just need time."

"Time's up, girl. You had plenty of time and plenty of opportunities before. Now give me the bag." Cece snatches the bag firmly.

"Let go! Let go!" Abby yells out as Cece pulls harder and harder. The bag rips, and Abby falls to the ground.

Cece hovers over her with such anger, an anger Abby has never seen before. "You're not going anywhere. Get over it!"

Abby jumps to her feet, chest-to-chest with Cece. "Try me!" she says, locking eyes with Cece's as her crystal starts glowing bright. The power from the necklace courses through her, and Abby ascends from her body in an out-of-body experience, looking down at them both. When she returns to herself, Cece is paused in time by Abby herself.

She puffs up her chest, high on her advantage, but as the last drops of power drain away, she breaks with tears rolling down her face, feeling more unwanted than ever. She backs away and walks past her, giving one final look at Cece. "I'm sorry, I really am. We are all in danger. I wish you would understand," Abby says to Cece's paused body before making her way down the hall. Turning at the top of the stairs, she looks once more at Cece and whispers goodbye for the last time. Her feet carry her full speed down the stairs and out the front door with no intention of turning back as time resumes once again.

CHAPTER SEVEN

Red Necklace

Abby walks aimlessly around town, minutes turning to hours, and a large part of the day has passed. Abby reflects to herself, upset and angry, with Cece for degrading her, and she feels more like a nobody. Throughout all the years living with Cece and her being so distant toward her, she realizes maybe Cece never liked her, and Abby is better off without her.

She stumbles upon a dead end, facing the dense woods. Abby somehow knows Friend is in there. "Friend! Are you in there?" She pauses, waiting for a response, anything, but nothing. "I know you're in there," she says to herself. Abby gives it another try. "Show me where you are!" Abby looks down at her necklace. Nothing happens. She sighs in disbelief that Friend, a monster, wanted to show himself so badly but now shuts himself away.

"This might be the last time I will ever see you. I don't know if you know, but I'm leaving Morgantown, and well…I think, this time, it's for good. There is a family who wants to take care of me somewhere far from here." She searches the tree line for a sign of him. "I know you don't want to hear from me now, but time is running out. I am extremely sorry for not taking the time to see what you were trying to show me. I know you've been laying out clues for me so I can better understand you. Friend, I may not know much about you from what I've learned, but to be honest, I have learned more about myself and what friendship really means in a short time. I don't want to go away without you." She has so much to learn but is being ignored and pushed away. "I need to know what I am to you!" Frustration builds within her; furious she's not hearing anything back. "If I called you Friend, then why are you not being a friend back to me?"

She unlatches her necklace and holds it in her hand. "I guess this is goodbye," she says while raising her arm up high in a fist. "You can have this back!" And she throws the necklace into the woods with no hesitation, hitting the branches and crunching dead leaves.

A sudden rush of wind circles around her. She touches her chest, and the necklace is back on her neck. She takes it off again. She moves to throw it, but there's nothing in her hands. The necklace is back on her neck once more, and Abby groans, frustrated. "I am sick and tired of your games, Friend. I am running out of time, and you aren't taking me seriously!"

She takes off the necklace for the third time, pulling her hand back, but a hand grips hers, stopping her from throwing. She can hear groans and clicks. "Friend, is that you?" She waits for more of a sign, then she hears it, a long grunt with the calming sound of the ticking noise, reassuring her he's there. She opens her hand, and the necklace is once again out of her hand and back on her neck, glowing bright. She turns around, and seeing that it is really Friend, she wraps him in a huge hug, catching him by surprise as he stands perfectly still. "I am so sorry I didn't believe in you. I want to remember everything we have done together."

Friend sighs while embracing her affection.

She tears up with happiness. "Is it true? Was it you giving me clues?"

Friend releases Abby, holding her back so she can see him shake his head no.

"No?" Abby looks at Friend, confused.

He gives another slow shake of his head.

"There was a man in Court Square, and he said some things about you being the monster and killing us all and the end is near."

Friend puts his hand on his chest, just like the statue the Eldest Elder described.

"Protection?"

He nods yes, then points at himself and to the necklace, symbolizing he is part of the necklace.

"I know this is you, but why can't I remember?"

Friend turns away, as if trying to not look at Abby, and begins to walk back into the woods. "Wait! I need to know why...why me?" Friend stops, his head drooping down, and stands there with his back facing her. A long pause of silence stretches between them with Abby looking around, making sure no one is around, awaiting the answer. A brisk, cold wind blows in the air, moving Abby's hair in a wild dance. The gust passes through her, giving her chills, and he looks up at the sky, still and silent.

"Is the portal coming to bring you back to Purity?"

He nods, clenching a fist in anger, still looking up, groaning. His clenched palm glows bright with Abby's necklace responding in turn.

"What do you want me to do?" He looks down with his back still facing her. "What can I do? I may not remember you, but there has to be something I can do to help. You came to me wounded, looking for help, and I helped you then. I need to know what you need me to do, please."

Friend sighs, releasing his clenched hand, and the glow dims in his palm. He turns now, facing her.

"I need to know more. There is so much I still don't know. The Eldest Elder said there is going to be a portal opening in Court Square. Last time, a monster came out of it named Buru, who you know from your home planet. But the homeless man went further, and he said your fight covered Morgantown with fire and ash, and everyone died. I've seen it with you, but everyone else in Morgantown is clueless to the fact it even happened. Did it—did that really happen?"

Friend nods yes.

"Can I help you in any way, so fire and ash don't happen?"

Friend shakes his head no.

To Abby, he looks sad and defeated, all limp, but before she can ask him another question, Friend snaps his fingers. Abby appears in front of the brownstone, a sign from Friend that this is not Abby's war to fight. It is dark and close to the meeting time with her new family. She looks up at her old home and gives off a deep sigh as she thinks of Cece. Abby feels bad for lashing out but knows it's too late to meet her new, potential parents. She can't start a new chapter without closing this one with Friend.

Abby knows Friend's intention is for her to leave him alone and for him to finish what he started, but she just can't let go. Something feels off, and she thinks the homeless man was right. Maybe the end is near, and maybe Friend is trying to fix the outcome. It is a hard decision to make, to allow Friend to do what he feels is right without her so she can live her life with Cece or in another potential home.

Wings rustle above her, so she looks up. Ping shuffles back and forth on the electrical wire, looking down at Abby. "What do you think I should do?" she asks him. Ping looks at her, as if he couldn't care less. "What do I do, what do I do?" Abby paces in front of the brownstone, takes in a deep breath. "Friend, please show me where I can find you." Her necklace points straight up at Ping. "You want me to follow Ping?" He just sits there, not looking like he's going to move anytime soon. "Well, come on then. Go, move, do something." But he doesn't move.

Not wanting to be too loud and catch any attention from inside, Abby picks up a small rock and throws it, barely missing him. He wakes up, flustered, and begins to fly away. She runs after him, trying to keep up with Ping as he swerves left and right, taking sharp turns.

What feels like hours but is likely only minutes passes as Abby is running out of breath. Her energy is depleted, and her legs are ready to give out, but her mind and will push her forward. Right when she wants to call it quits, a shadow of a man curled up comes into view. He lies on the ground in a cubby of a storefront entrance. Wrapped in a dirty box with his legs sticking out, he sobs, "Sarah, Jacob, Molly…Sarah, Jacob…Molly."

Ping continues to fly as she slows down to catch her breath. She inches over to the mumbling man and listens in on him speaking the names Sarah, Jacob, Molly. Trying to get closer, she trips on a bottle lying on the sidewalk, kicking it toward him. It skips across the hard cement ground, making loud clinks and tinkle sounds in the dead-asleep town.

His mumbling stops immediately. Sitting up, he peeks his head out and, at the sight of Abby, becomes shocked and afraid. "Oh, no, it's you!" he yells with a tremble in his voice. She stumbles back as she realizes it's the homeless man from Court Square. "Stay away. I want no business with you or the monster you run around with." The man curls up into a ball, hiding his face with the dirty cardboard box sheet. "Please, please go, leave me be," the man pleads.

She walks closer as he whimpers underneath the cardboard box, reciting the names. "How do you know of him?" she asks the man. "Why should we remember that day? You are the only one who knows of the monster and that day."

"I stayed in the dome. The monster turned back time, leaving me like this where Molly…Molly." The man takes the box off his head and points at Abby. "You don't remember what that monster is. You don't remember that day." He shakes his dirty, wrapped hand at her, smiling insanely.

"The names you were saying—"

The man starts rocking in place. "Why me?" he wails. His mood morphs to anger, punching the side of his own head. "That monster did this to me!" He turns his crazy stare on Abby. "You... you were here. Let me jog your memory. The portal opened while your monster friend was fighting what came out of it, leveling the whole town to fire and ash as they fought, and everyone out of the dome burnt like..." The man takes a deep breath, then continues, "But your monster friend was winning and winning well. I was there, and you were fighting alongside him, calling him your friend and calling whatever came out of that portal Buru."

"Buru!"

"That's what you called it, whatever it is. Then, during the fight, something happened, and that friend of yours lost its cool, knocking the monster Buru back into the portal and, poof, went back in time. Everyone else went back in time and got young but not me. I stayed my age, and everyone forgot that day...and me. That changed my life forever."

"Can I ask how?" Abby says.

The man hesitates, making a long humming noise, clenching his lip, wanting to speak but holding himself back. "Sarah, Jacob, Molly, umm..." The man pauses, looking at his dirty nails and sighing to himself. "Seven years since this all happened. That's why I predict the end is near. See, girl, you and everyone else went back in time where I have not. I am the only one who remembers what happened that night and the only one who survived the fight. My family is gone, walks past me every day, not knowing it's me. They think I left them, vanishing in thin air, but I didn't. I sit here every day, watching them grow, watching them live their life without their father."

"Those names you repeat, are those the names of your family?"

"Yes, Sarah and Jacob are my kids, and Molly is my wife. Molly Leland."

A long silence looms as Abby takes in what the man is saying. "You're her missing husband!"

He groans, defeated, "No one believes me."

She feels bad how his life changed because of Friend, but she can't think of an explanation on why Friend did it. Abby wants to know more about the portal and the fight that leveled Morgantown to nothingness. She remembers back, standing outside school, looking over the inflamed town and the glowing dome around Court Square, as if that area was worth being protected.

Her necklace begins to glow again, pointing down the street. "I'm sorry about what you have gone through, but I believe this has a bigger meaning than you think," she says to the man as he rocks himself, making the same noise as Friend, chanting the names of his family. She knows he is still listening, so Abby continues, "I think you were brought here to remember that day to tell me what I need to know, even though it raised even more questions I may never learn the answers to. There is a reason for this, and I know it. I just hope I can one day help you."

"You did enough damage, girl. The end is near, and I hope for good this time so I don't have to relive this life again." He continues his ticking noises while sounding defeated, what was left of his sanity lost.

She feels bad leaving the man to lie there all alone, so Abby asks, "What is your name?"

The man looks through her, answering, "My name is Joey, Joey Leland. Now please run off, little girl."

Her necklace tugs on her neck, glowing and pointing down Main Street to a sign or a clue. She runs down the street. The town is empty with not a car in sight, her surroundings dark and eerie. The necklace makes a sharp left, whipping her neck violently with it. "Ouch!" Abby yells out loud from the chain rubbing into her skin. The necklace points right before the light turns off, and the crystal falls back in place as normal.

She looks around her surroundings, noticing she is next to her high school, and the necklace last pointed at the school grounds in the back of the field. She knows the necklace brought her here for a reason but is afraid to trespass in the dark. Abby looks up and down the street with the eerie feeling she is being watched. She knows the way in, behind the bleachers where the hole is cut in between the two overgrown bushes. Abby walks around the school, checking over her shoulder from time to time. She still feels like she is being watched, but she pushes forward.

Inside the grounds, she finds the hole in the fence wide open. She gives one more look around but hears and sees nothing. Taking a deep, calming breath, she squeezes her body through, barely fitting through the small opening, and crawls under the school bleachers. She squints around in the dark, trying to find her way, tripping and stumbling over bottles and cans; the ground is littered with cigarette butts and other teenage contraband. She finds an opening in the bleachers and slips out into the open.

She crosses to the other side of the field, heading toward the edge of the woods where she last entered. Her eyes drift up to the tops of the trees, only seeing the silhouette of the branches illuminated by the stars and moon above, still and quiet. Behind her in the distance, she stares at the sidewalk streetlight and sees how far she is from feeling safe. Emptiness and loneliness fill her up. She holds herself with a cold chill running down her spine.

She takes a cold, deep breath, the heavy push of air a cloud in the night chill. "Friend, I know you're in there. Please come out, come on! I know you're in there. You are the one who reached out to me with the necklace. I'm not here to play games." Abby pauses, hoping she can hear any response from the other side of the woods, but there is nothing. "Come on!" Cold and frustrated, she knows this is the last chance she has left. She tries one more time and a little louder. "Friend, I know you're—"

"Fake!" is yelled from behind her, making her jump and spin around to see Rachel and Jennifer in the darkness of the field with a couple of their groupies. Jennifer looks mad, staring right into Abby's eyes. "You heard me, Abby. Fake, not real. You see, no one wants you. You destroyed my life, expelling me over a stupid video. You're going to get what you deserve."

Jennifer storms up to Abby, unaware it was her own sister who ratted her out. Jennifer pushes Abby back, closer to the edge of the woods, but she doesn't go down. She holds her ground, standing strong.

Rachel steps in. "Jennifer, I think we should go. Mom should be here soon to pick us up."

The other girls shush Rachel, waiting for Jennifer to fight Abby. "Whose side are you on?"

"Sorry," Rachel says, putting her head down.

Jennifer continues, "Did you hear that, Abby? Our mom is going to pick us up. That's something you don't have and will never experience." Abby stares at Jennifer with her fist clenched, not saying a single word but staring deep into her eyes. Jennifer gets agitated, fast. "What are you going to do, Abby?" She pushes her a second time.

"Again, Jennifer, harder," one of the girls says, provoking her.

Abby squares her shoulders, holding her ground and showing Jennifer she is not going anywhere. Jennifer pushes her farther back now, up against a tree. "Who's going to help you out here in the dark? I thought to myself, how I can get back at you…well, I guess I'll start here." She smacks Abby across the face, but Abby stays composed, locking eyes with her.

Headlights in the school parking lot catch Abby's eye. Rachel looks as well. "Come on, Jennifer. Mom's here."

Jennifer punches Abby in the stomach, knocking all the air out of her, leaving Abby to kneel and catch her breath. Jennifer backs up. "Yeah, let's go. I think we are done here, right, girls?"

"Oh, shoot, it was just getting exciting," one of the girls says behind Rachel.

Jennifer walks past Rachel, purposely bumping into her. Rachel looks at Abby, remorse twisting her features for a second, then follows Jennifer and the group.

Abby watches them walk away as she tries catching her breath, but she hears someone else behind her in the woods. "Friend?" Abby says, gaining strength to get back up. Her necklace faintly glows once with the groaning clicks of Friend right behind her, hiding, and she knows now she is safe. "Okay, Friend, let's play a game."

Friend groans deep, agreeing.

She takes in a big breath. "Hey...bitch," Abby calls out, catching her breath again.

Jennifer turns around with her group oohing over Abby's words. "Excuse me!" Jennifer yells, marching back to Abby, while Rachel struggles to hold her sister back with no luck.

"To answer your question, the one who would help me, that would be my friend. He's going to help me," Abby says, now standing up, chest out with her necklace glowing. She's trying so hard to be strong, knowing this time she has back up from Friend, who is still hiding in the woods.

Jennifer walks up to Abby. "Do you think you're funny?" she says, snarling and clenching her fist, ready to fight.

Abby smiles, knowing she has the upper hand.

Jennifer takes a small step back, caught off guard by Abby's confidence. "What is so funny, Foster Trash?"

"Come on, Jennifer. Mom is waiting," Rachel pleads, not wanting a fight.

"Shut up!" Jennifer snaps back. "So, where's your friend? Let me guess, imaginary?"

Abby says nothing, just smiling larger.

"Oh, you poor, poor deadbeat, a waste of air no one loves," Jennifer says with a fake sympathetic voice.

"Oooh!" comes from the girls behind Jennifer, pushing her to insult more.

Just when Jennifer has a snub poised on her tongue, Friend cuts her off with a deep groan right behind Abby. The girls' faces drop as fear sets in.

"Oh, I almost forgot to introduce my friend. How rude of me," Abby says sarcastically to Jennifer as she starts to step back, looking into the darkness. She goes on, "And I forgot to tell you, Jennifer, he does not like to be called imaginary, but he likes to play games. Come on out, Friend, I need your help."

Abby's necklace brightly glows, dead autumn leaves rustling and branches crackling in the woods. Jennifer falls in fear, and Rachel wastes no time running with the other girls to the car waiting for them in the parking lot.

Abby hovers over Jennifer. "Every day, you treat me like I'm a nobody just so others will like you. I was your puppet, your tool, and I took it every—single—day! You never felt bad about what you were doing as I was just taking the hits. If there is one thing I have learned in the last couple of days, it's that it's okay to be different, and sometimes, it's that one friend who can show you that. That one friend who makes you feel protected, no matter what. I may not have parents or a family like you, and I'm okay with that. Sometimes, you just have to let life live itself out and let time guide you." Friend emerges as a black silhouette, standing right behind Abby. "This is my friend, and he is more of a friend than what you have."

She looks up at Friend for reassurance with his tall shadow nodding back and putting his fist on his chest with one loud beat.

"You ready, Friend?" she says with a smirk on her face, and Friend makes clicking noises, putting his hand on her shoulder and pushing her behind him.

Jennifer screams franticly, trying to get up but stumbling over her own feet. Friend flicks his wrist, and his palm turns blue. Jennifer sprints down the field, not turning back, straight to the parked car with Rachel and the others climbing on top of each other. He watches her go.

Abby walks up to Friend. "Thank you for helping me. You're a true friend, Friend." He puts his hand on her head, bringing her closer to him. Abby hugs his leg, comforted, like this is where she belongs.

Friend groans, nudging his head toward Jennifer and the car, as if saying, "Let's go." Jennifer and her gang have finally piled into the car, screams of "Go, go, go!" echoing back to them.

Abby is taken aback. "But they would see you."

Friend nods, puts his fist on his chest as the other hand glows.

With time slowed down, Abby takes one step forward, and she is by herself but much closer to the car—small steps are much larger when time is slowed down. She turns around, and Friend's shadowed body down the field is beside Abby in a blink. "So when you slow time, it makes us faster than time, just like in the book?" she says to him as he replies with a quick nod, and extends a hand out for Abby to take. Another step brings her right in front of Jennifer's mother's car.

Staring through the windshield, Abby investigates the backseat of the car, Rachel and the other girls have their faces pressed to the window, pointing out into the field in fear. Abby walks up to the driver's side window where Jennifer is yelling at her mother, who looks utterly confused.

Looking closer, she sees they are not fully stopped in time but slowed down. Jennifer's mouth moves, but it's too slow to make out what she is saying. Her eyes grow large, locking with Abby's, and the mother's mood changes to shocked, her gaze focused straight ahead on Friend, who's standing in front of the car, grunting to catch her attention.

"Friend, what are you going to do?"

He snaps his fingers, putting the car in motion right at him. The car brakes squeal to a stop inches from his legs. Friend pounds on the hood of the car with his fist and walks over to the driver's side. He leans his forearm on the roof, tapping the window with the other hand. He stands poised yet flamboyant, the car and surroundings once again slowed in time, as Friend incites fear into the ones who bother and intimidate his friend, Abby.

Everyone in the car, even Jennifer's mother, scream hysterically, and Abby just has the urge to laugh. Friend looks over at her, making a gesture with his hand as if he is saying they're talking too much, giving a smile, and Abby smiles back like this is all normal. He mimics their slowed-down, blood-curdling screams, then, bringing time back to normal pace, opens his jaw in a grin. The skin over his eyes and mouth glow blue, making the scream louder and scarier. He glances back at Abby for a reaction, clicking and growling all in good fun.

Her gaze is drawn elsewhere, and she releases a startled gasp. "Friend, what is going on with the necklace?" Her necklace turns a deep red, dimming and pushing on her chest, shining ominously under her chin.

A bright beam of light shines in her eyes, blinding her before moving to Friend. She rubs her eyes, her vision clearing to a sheriff's patrol car spotlight pointing right at Friend. *He must have heard the screams*, Abby thinks to herself.

The sheriff exits his vehicle, drawing his weapon and aiming it at Friend. "Freeze! Don't move, whatever the hell you are!" the sheriff yells at Friend. "Girl, step away from the monster." He reaches over to his shoulder, talking low into the walkie-talkie. Friend stands upright at the provocation.

"Friend, we have to go now," she says nervously while, in the distance, more sirens wail, coming from all angles. "Now they know who you are and will try to stop you when the portal opens. This is not good, and we need to go now."

He agrees as the sheriff yells back, "Don't move!"

Friend takes a step forward, distracting the officer while waving his hands, glowing blue, freezing time as the lights still flicker on the patrol car. He turns, holding on to Abby's necklace and cradling it in his hand as it still blinks red. He looks disgusted as he closes his hand over the crystal and deeply sighs. Abby knows this is the beginning of the end.

"What's happening, Friend?"

Friend just stands there, shaking his head.

"We need to go to Court Square."

Friend waves his finger side to side while shaking his head, pointing to the ground, telling her to stay here.

"No? I can't do that to you. Can we go back in time before this happened?" He shakes his head.

"Why?"

Friend points to Abby's necklace, still flickering red.

"Can we go back to before *this* happened?" she asks, looking down at the necklace.

Friend once again shakes his head and points to his wrist, tapping twice.

"No time? How much time do we have to prepare?" Abby pauses, hit with a realization. "Who is Buru to you? Is my necklace signaling fire and ash is near?"

Friend nods.

It's mildly reassuring that Joey, the homeless man, was right about the portal, the fight, and the destruction. "Friend, I want you to show me that day. What happened that day that made everything go wrong?"

Friend sighs while shaking his head, pointing at his wrist, indicating no time.

She stomps the ground and crosses her arms, frustrated over not getting the answers she wants. "You called me out here, but for what? To play around and get caught, was that it?" she snaps. "I'm starting to feel like you're taking me for an endless ride."

Friend looks down, sad, and reaches out his hand awkwardly to console her, but she shuts him down.

"Tell me everything now before any more time runs out because I know you are leaving for good."

Friend gets mad, roaring in Abby's face until all the air leaves his lungs with his hands, mouth, and eye sockets all glowing bright, letting out all his anger and slowly dimming down his own powers. Wind from his breath blows onto her face. She snarls back to Friend's face, showing she is not afraid of his frustrating threat.

"Then when? When can you tell me?!"

He aggressively reaches into his blazer pocket, pulling out a dirty and worn journal, the same journal he was trying to put into her backpack when he pushed her into the puddle.

Flipping through the pages as they get bloodier and the pages stick to each other, he reaches the very end, ripping out the last page of the book. The page is stained with old blood on the corners. She grabs the ripped page and begins to read:

Today is the day. We both can feel it, the day we have been training for. We may not know the end results, but hopefully, Friend can finally tackle his past once and for all. Friend has treated me like one of his own, and I have learned so much in the last seven long years living in that treehouse. I'm going to miss him and all of the missions we have gone through in that time. I can be nothing but grateful for his protection and for him teaching me how to take care of myself, even when moments got tough. He was and always will be here for me, and there is no parent out there who would ever treat me so fairly. I give him my life to help him in this battle.

Abby can't read any further because the pencil writing is worn, and blood and mud cover most of the bottom of the page. "Seven years," she murmurs, reality setting in. "You took care of me?"

Friend nods.

"You raised me for seven years. But how have I been living in a foster home with Cece this whole time since I was seven?"

He shakes his head, tapping his wrist. There's not enough time to get into that one.

"When we were in that yard, were those my parents?"

He shakes his head no.

"How did you first meet me? Did you know my real parents? Are they still alive?"

Friend points at his wrist, tapping in a rush.

"Okay, I trust you. I'm ready."

He beats his chest with a fist before snapping his fingers. Everything around them flashes, and they come to in her bedroom. Her heart sinks to her stomach. "No, no, no. I don't trust this. When I said we need to go, I didn't mean my room." She runs to the door and closes it, forgetting the loud squeal it makes when closed too quickly, alerting Cece to her presence. "Friend, you need to go and hide *now*!" In a panic, she opens her closet, pushing

Friend inside, contorting his tall body with his knees to his chest. She manages to close the closet door.

"Abby, open up right now!" Cece yells from the other side of the door, violently rattling the doorknob.

Abby knows she is in deep trouble, missing the meeting with her new parents. She takes a deep breath, readying herself for what may happen next.

The door opens to Cece shaking her head, her eyes bold with anger, piercing through her magnified glasses and making her eyes much larger and more intimidating than usual. "You have no respect for what you really have, do you? Don't make this my problem that you lost a family you could've called your own." Cece tries to hold back, stuttering over her words as her anger leaves her speechless, but she can't control herself. She raises her hand up high, swinging toward Abby's face. Abby closes her eyes, ready to be hit, but nothing happens.

Friend stands behind Cece, snatching her wrist at the last second. Cece looks at Abby, confused and surprised as she tries to release her arm, not looking at what is behind her. Abby's necklace begins to glow.

Friend makes his groan-like clicks behind Cece, lifting her straight up in the air and spinning her around to face him. He groans in her face, his eyes glowing blue, just like with the man at the junkyard house.

Cece screams in fear. Abby stands still, her own anger at Cece raging, not planning to intervene. Friend grips her wrist tighter as her time speeds up and she starts aging quickly. She cries out in pain but receives no reaction from Abby, who's zoning out and repeating Cece's words in her head.

Friend screams in Cece's face, louder with his power running through him.

Abby's necklace glows as she snaps out of her anger, knowing now it's not worth Cece getting injured over Abby's own actions. "Wait, put her down. I don't think that's a good idea."

Friend ignores her as Cece gets even older, as if on her final breath. Friend is killing her timeline. She walks to his side to get his attention, reaching up to his cold hand. A pulse of energy runs through her, and a bright light blinds her, not helped by the sudden appearance of sunlight in her eyes.

Abby quickly looks around, as she is no longer in her room. The sunshine pours into the living room's bay windows with the room looking much different. The furniture is unwrapped from its plastic, and the environment feels fresh and alive. The walls are covered with framed photos Abby has never seen before. She glances over to one of the photos of a much younger Cece with Mr. Carter, looking very much in love as they wrap around a little girl who looks remarkably similar to Abby herself. The same little girl in the photo that was on Cece's nightstand.

"Friend...Cece...?" Abby yells but with no response. Conversations are heard from outside; Abby runs to the front door.

CHAPTER EIGHT

You're So Strong

Abby looks up and down the block as she stands in front of the brownstone, noticing how clean and new Morgantown looks with less dirt and rust. Parked cars on the road and in driveways are older, and the people walking the streets wear clothes from the early '70s. By touching Friend while using his powers on Cece, she can see what he sees in her timeline, moments she's lived, and who she is as a person; seeing if she is pure. "This must be an important time," Abby says to herself as an old-fashioned, yellow school bus drives down the street, stopping in front of the brownstone with its yellow lights flashing.

The bus door opens, and a young girl jumps down the steps. Her backpack weighs her down as it swings side to side, and she struggles not to fall, but it doesn't put down her spirits. She wears a medical mask over her face and a bandana over her pale head. Her eyes are large and wide, and her round cheekbones suggest a smile hidden under her mask. Abby realizes it's the same girl she saw in Cece's room.

As the school bus pulls away, the front door of the brownstone behind Abby opens, and she turns, shocked to see a much younger Cece, standing more upright, adjusting her large glasses, and most of all, wearing a huge smile on her face. Her gaze passes right through her, as Abby is merely an invisible bystander in Cece's timeline.

"Mama!" The small girl runs up the steps as fast as she can with her oversized backpack swinging and whipping her around, so excited to be what seems to be home. She is visibly sick, but that's not breaking her smile as she runs into Cece's arms.

Cece embraces her in a warm hug, laughing and smiling. "Oh, Amelia, you're getting so strong. Your hugs are getting so tight I can barely breathe."

Hudson Carter emerges from the house, wearing his suit and holding his briefcase, smiling behind Cece. "Hey, can I take a photo with you and mom to add to our scrapbook?"

"Yes, Father!" the little girl, Amelia, says, delighted, as he takes their photo, the bright flash of his camera blinding them both in their smiles.

He kneels down, opening his briefcase to return his camera. "This is what I'm selling next." He pulls out a collection of hair combs for men and women; Amelia's eyes light up.

"Wow, that's so cool. Everyone needs a comb...except me." Her mood shifts to sadness.

"No, Amelia, you're not seeing the bigger picture. Here, take one. I sell things to make money for your medicine, and with that medicine, it can one day help your hair grow."

She shoots up with excitement. "How many do we have to sell? Can I help?"

"Oh, so you want to be my business partner. Well, then we're going to have to get you a suit—I know a man who can help us with that—and we're going to have to sell a lot of these combs. Are you up for the challenge?"

"I sure am!" They all smile happily and laugh together as they go into the brownstone.

Abby follows, walking into the same brownstone she grew up in that looks completely different inside. She looks around at all the pictures everywhere of younger Cece and the little girl, Amelia. In the pictures, the little girl looks very similar to Abby with her curly hair and big, wide eyes. There are balloons and cards all over, some reading, "Get well soon, Amelia!" and "You can beat this!"

Time passes within the room. Balloons deflate, and the room gets dim, and flowers pop up around the living room, giving more support. Time slows down to the sound of whimpering coming from what would be Abby's room, the door open and the light spilling into the dark hallway. Abby walks in and sees Cece, Mr. Carter, and a doctor hovering over the bedside of Amelia. Cece sits on the side of the bed, holding her hand as Amelia slips in and out of consciousness. Medications litter the nightstand, along with love and support from cards and more flowers. The only sound is Cece weeping her name, but no response comes from the girl.

The doctor checks her pulse. "She's gone. I'm sorry," he says as Cece buries her face in Amelia's motionless chest, hugging her tight.

Mr. Carter's hand rests on Cece's back, lowering his head to cover his sadness. "My baby girl," he says to himself.

"You are still strong, Amelia, so very strong," Cece whispers to her, trying to fight back her tears.

Everything in the room quickens into a time-lapse as the doctor leaves, and younger Cece stays, pacing as people flood in and out of the bedroom, saying their final goodbyes to young Amelia. Someone from the funeral home takes her body away. Cece stays behind, still pacing in the room as the sun sets and the bedroom gets dark, and she sits on the bed, looking out the window, weeping. The bedroom turns to black with flashes of lightning and heavy rumbles of thunder.

The scene changes to a small cemetery with rain pouring on the casket. Cece stands alone, dressed in black. Her umbrella in one hand and a handkerchief in the other, dabbing the tear-smudged makeup from her eyes, she says her final goodbyes to the love of her life. "My little girl. You fought with a smile, a smile I will never forget, and your father would say the same. It was hard for him to come to terms that you are not with us, but I know he will always remember the good times we had as a whole. Like what you said, pieces are just fragments of a whole, and you can have one without the other. I might feel alone, but I'll always have you here," she says, demonstrating two halves of a heart with her hands, putting them together to make one whole heart as tears fall from her eyes. "I love you, and I will miss you."

As Abby spectates under a tree, Friend appears behind Cece, putting his hand on her shoulder as if he is sharing in Cece's pain. The rain and wind get heavier. Abby walks over as Cece watches Amelia being lowered into her final resting place, clueless that Abby and Friend are there. Friend stands side by side with her like he too is saying his final goodbyes.

"She should not have her life taken from her, not like this," Abby says. "I didn't know anything about Cece's life, especially not this, but I can see why she was so stern. She lost someone so close to her, her own daughter. She was nice enough to take me into her home, and I'm not mad at her for being who she is."

Friend agrees.

"Can we go back and make this not happen?"

Friend shakes his head no, catching Abby by surprise as he snaps his fingers. He can see events further into her timeline that Abby should see.

Abby flashes back to the brownstone inside the living room, not what Abby remembers. There are no pictures of Amelia to be seen. She walks into the dining room where Cece, older than she was at the cemetery, sits by herself quietly. She's holding a picture of Amelia when the phone rings. Cece stands up slowly, looking depressed as she shuffles her feet to answer the phone.

"Yes, who is this?" she says with the attitude Abby is far too familiar with. The voice begins to speak on the other end, Cece's body springing up, surprised. "Oh, yes, yes, yes. What would you need from me? Okay...Okay. When would this start? I'm as ready as I could be.

Okay, o—Today, that quick? Twelve o'clock, that's in twenty minutes...Oh, no, no, no, I'm ready, yes. Okay then, see you soon." Cece hangs up the phone softly, looking back at the photo of Amelia. "Well, a new chapter of my life just opened," she says to the photo as she picks it up to put it away.

The time-lapse passes, stopping as the doorbell rings. Cece swings the door open to a woman standing alone. "Hello, Cecilia, is it okay if I come in and talk to you first?"

"Sure, come in, come in, right this way." Cece leads the woman into the living room where they both take a seat.

"Cecilia, I have known you my whole life, and I am so happy to see you are moving forward. There's something with the story of this little girl I don't understand, and I hope you're up for the challenge."

"Yes, I am. What's her story?"

"Well, that's the thing, you see. We just found her on the orphanage's steps, and she seems pretty clueless and unaware of what happened to her or where she even came from. We're trying to figure out who she is and where we can bring her, but it doesn't look like that's going to happen. It seems like she's, well, you know, one of those kids that some parents just don't want, I guess. So we were wondering if you can take care of her to maybe see if she can get her memory back in a home setting rather than a foster care setting."

"Okay, but I don't see what's so challenging about that," Cece says with confusion.

"That's not the challenge, Cecilia. I know what you've gone through with your daughter, but this girl," the woman sits forward, resting a hand on top of Cece's, "she looks just like Amelia. This can maybe be a healing process for you."

"Like Amelia?" Cece startles, as if shocked with electricity. "It's been so long since I heard someone say her name."

"She goes by the name Abby. Maybe she'll bring you happiness, Cecilia, just like your daughter."

Cece cautiously nods, her fingertips tingling as her nerves set in.

The woman reaches over to a walkie-talkie strapped to her side. "Bring her in," she says. Cece's eyes drift to the front door expectantly. "How old is she?"

"She says she's seven years old."

Cece gives a nod as the front door swings open. Young, seven-year-old Abby and a man in a suit stand in the doorway, her big eyes looking right at Cece, shy as her eyes wander.

"Amelia?" she says to herself, shaking her head, trying not to relive the time when Amelia was alive.

A man in a black suit walks Abby in closer. "Abby, this is where you're going to stay for a little bit. Are you okay with that?"

Abby is shy as she nods her head, and she tries to hide her face with a dirty, pink stuffed rabbit.

The woman next to Cece asks her, "Are you okay with this, Cecilia?"

Cece cracks a smile—she can't take her eyes off Abby—and she nods, then says, "But I don't want to replace my Amelia."

The room turns black with the sound of a snap.

Abby is back in her room with Friend and no Cece. "Where is she? Where did she go?" Friend raises up a finger to his mouth, telling Abby to be quiet, and points at her door. "She's out there… Is she okay?"

He nods. "Does she remember you?"

He shakes his head no.

A pause follows as they hear Cece walk down the hall, completely clueless they both are in the room.

"Friend, I can't be doing this anymore. If you don't show me what is going on, we are putting ourselves more at risk. I can't be running around like this any longer."

Friend points at his wrist.

"Time! But we have time to come back here," Abby forcefully whispers to him.

He reaches inside his blazer as she hears sirens wail through her window, making Abby paranoid they're looking for her and Friend. He presents the journal, the same notebook he ripped the last page out of, and hands it to Abby. It's badly beaten and weathered with blood stains on the back, bleeding onto the pages. She rubs her finger across the front cover, feeling the words deeply engraved in its pages.

"This was mine? Why did you hide this from me? This can answer a lot of questions."

He sighs, reaching back into his blazer and producing her stuffed rabbit. Her necklace glows red again. He gets on one knee, hugging Abby tight before stepping away from her.

"Wait, where are you going?"

Friend points out the window, and his hand starts to glow.

"So, this is goodbye forever. I mean, seven years to this day, right? People said a portal was going to open in Court Square, so tell me the truth. Is this how you're going to say goodbye? Without telling me what is going on?" Her arms drop loosely to her side, defeated. Friend's hand stops glowing and drops, his stance mirroring hers. They are both quiet, not knowing what to say or do next.

Bang, bang, bang! "Morgantown Sheriff's Department, open up!"

Abby runs to the window, seeing a patrol car and two officers at the front door. She turns back to Friend. "We need to leave. You aren't safe here."

Friend lights up his hand, getting ready to go.

Abby runs over, grabbing his hand. "Take me with you. Please, I'm not safe here either. They will ask me questions. Questions I can't answer." Catching him off guard, she tightens her hold. "I need you to let me know the whole truth."

Friend tries to pull her away, but she holds too tight as the officers' footsteps barrel down the hallway outside her door. Her bedroom door opens, and the two officers burst into her room, guns drawn, Friend and Abby vanishing just in time.

One officer says into his walkie-talkie, "All clear. Hostage is not here."

Cece walks in. "Hostage? I called because she didn't come home after dark. What is going on?"

"Just a moment, ma'am." Over the walkie-talkie, the officer reports, "Arrived on scene. No sign of monster or child."

The people in Morgantown attend a community gathering where they decorate Court Square for Halloween. The people gather with hay bales, carved pumpkins, and their spooky props, and they are bundled up in the frigid and raw temperatures as it dips lower into the night. Everything seems to be normal until Friend and Abby appear out of thin air at the entrance of Court Square. Screams of shock and horror over a monster and a small girl appearing out of nowhere pierce the air. The people scramble in all directions.

Friend ignores them as he strides ahead of her. He stops in front of the statue, resting his hand on the base. She moves to run after him, but a sudden gust of wind rushes across her face, and she ducks. A second later, she realizes it's Ping, rushing past Abby and right to Friend, landing on his shoulder.

She catches up to them, grabbing Friend's hand and holding it tight. "Is this where the portal will open…Buru and the fight?"

Friend grunts, nodding, taking his hand off the base, lingering on the words "For honor." He walks away toward the tall courthouse steps.

Sirens are heard all throughout Morgantown, and the red and blue lights illuminate the night sky. Friend jerks Abby's hand and sprints away as a voice yells, "Freeze! Let go of the girl!"

The two vanish as a loud bang rings out from one of the officer's guns, sparks hitting the ground where Friend and Abby last stood. They reappear at the top of the courthouse steps. Friend pushes Abby behind one of the large pillars to hide. Ping flies from Friend's shoulder to a statue behind Abby to watch like a fly on the wall.

"You're not supposed to be here!" Abigail's voice says in rage.

Her necklace glows red and, for the first time, remains a solid color. Friend puts his hand up, telling Abby to wait here.

"Please don't get hurt," she replies, concerned about his safety.

He stands up slowly and faces the police, grunting, extending his long, frail arms out, as if showing he is not a threat.

A voice comes from one of the officer's intercom, "Give us the girl and no one gets hurt. We don't want to harm you." Friend doesn't move, standing as if he too is a statue, stalling time.

"Wait!" Abby yells out, coming out from behind the pillar. "You can't do this. You can't act on something you don't understand."

The same voice blares over a police car speaker, "We need you to step away from the monster at once."

"He is here to save us, all of us. There is going to be a portal that opens here in the courtyard."

There's a pause as the officer considers this sudden supernatural turn of events but plays along. "Is it a threat to Morgantown, the portal?"

"What comes out of it is, not him. He is my friend, and I trust him."

Across the courtyard, the officers gather together, questioning the probability of a portal actually appearing. They shoot doubtful looks their way and remember a real-life monster is standing before them. The voice comes on over the speaker,

"Alright, girl, we will give you thirty minutes. If there is no portal, then we have no choice but to take action against the mon— your friend."

Abby has no other choice but to agree. She whispers to him, "How much longer? We don't have much time."

Friend sighs, shrugging his shoulders.

The minutes tick by, and she starts to worry as more officers arrive, heavily armed with guns, armor, and shields. One officer says, "Time's up." A red dot aims right at Friend's chest, but it does not faze him.

There are more police vehicles surrounding them, aiming their guns in Friend's direction. The headlights beam on them, and Friend and Abby both cover their eyes as their sense of sight is crippled. A loud bang rings out. Friend lets out a loud, threatening roar. She blinks the stars from her eyes and gasps at Friend holding his bleeding shoulder. They shot Friend. His hand glows over his wound, healing the bullet hole. Breathing angrily, he looks at his healed wound and whips his head around at the officers with all their guns pointing at him. His hands and eye sockets intensify in glow, readying himself to fight.

"No, don't hurt them," Abby yells out as she runs behind him, grabbing onto his leg, knowing what Friend is capable of.

"Hold your fire!" comes from an officer.

She holds on tight to Friend. "I don't want more people to get hurt. Can we go back in time so this doesn't happen? Is that possible?"

He puts a protective hand on her head, bringing her closer and releasing a rage-filled roar at the officers. His glare swings up to the sky as he hears a whipping hum in the distance.

Abby's necklace glows red again as she and the officers follow suit, trying to find out where the noise is coming from. During the distraction, the guns point their lasers at Friend's chest and face, dancing all over him, searching for the best spot to strike.

"No, don't!" Abby cries.

"Step away from the monster! You have 'til the count of three… men, ready!" She holds Friend's leg as tight as she can, her necklace still glowing red as guns cock and bullets slide into chambers. "Two…aim!"

"This is not what I want to happen. Friend, what do we do now? We can't wait any longer! They don't believe us," she cries, struggling to hold back her tears as she stuffs her face into Friend's leg. He stands his ground, still looking ahead, making sure Abby is behind him.

Friend takes in a heavy sigh, as he knows this is the end of a new beginning. He can feel the portal coming, making this the last time to show Abby the truth. Deep down inside, he wants to show Abby the truth, the truth of their friendship. A final gift to what she means to him and all of the pivotal moments they had together.

She holds Friend's leg even tighter, rubbing the tears running down her cheeks onto his pant leg. Friend suddenly shoves Abby back behind the pillar, away from harm's way and ready to fight. She hits the ground with a heavy thud, scrambling to repel herself off the ground to take cover.

"One…fire!"

Shots ring out, flashes from gun muzzles light up the courtyard as bullets fly toward them both. Friend puts out his hand, slowing down time while simultaneously creating an energy shield in front of him. The bullets fly into his shield, slowing down to a complete stop inches from his body. The officers empty their clips, and Friend twists his glowing hand, spinning the bullets around to face the police. The officers halt their shooting, in shock as Friend points his finger, shaping it as a gun and pulling the trigger. The bullets fly at them and make contact with the patrol cars and officers on the frontline. Officers fall one by one, intentionally struck in nonlethal areas of their bodies as a warning.

Abby closes her eyes tight, hearing the screams of immense pain coming from the officers in the courtyard. In a split second, the sound of Friend snapping his fingers silences the screams, pausing time, including Abby. He puts his guard down as an eerie silence looms, he looks over to Abby, who's hunched over with her back pressed to the courthouse pillar. Her chest is pressed to her knees and her fingers are plugging her ears to drown out the sounds of horror.

He knows his time is coming to an end but can't leave with the guilty conscience of her not understanding the impact he had on her life. Even though the Eldest Elder speaks the truth of her lack of memory, he feels like the time is right to show her. He walks over to Abby and places his cold thumb to her forehead, and her eyes abruptly open, glowing blue.

In an out-of-body experience, Abby opens her eyes, but she's not in the courtyard anymore. Instead, she's by herself in an endless, black, empty room. She looks around. "Hello?" The word echoes, sounding like it goes for miles as she wipes the tears away from her eyes. One tear drops to the floor, and her eyes follow its path down to her feet. "Friend!" Below her is a bird's-eye view of Court Square, Friend and herself on the courthouse steps. Time has stopped, and Abby's eyes are glowing blue. The officers still standing aim their guns, but their bullets hover in the air by Friend's power.

"Friend, can you hear me? Friend!" Abby calls out, banging against the floor. She glances around her, wondering, "What is this place?"

Friend looks up like he can hear her. He taps on his head, as if telling her she is in his mind, then taps on his wrist.

"Time? Your timeline? I don't think this is the right time for that."

He nods slowly as the floor starts moving beneath her, knocking her off balance, and her reality in Morgantown with Friend and the officers fades away to black.

A small, blue glow floating in the air flies over to Abby and stops in front of her. Warm heat radiates from the light as she reaches out, touching it with her finger. The light brightens, lightning-like roots branching out of it and forming into a body, Abby's body but slightly different. Her orb self has the cracked necklace on her neck, the same one Friend had in his hand when he came in through her bedroom window when she first met him. She stands face-to-face with herself, the orb mimicking her, as if they're both mirrors.

The orb smiles, puffing out her chest and crossing her fist over before flashing back into a little ball of light. "It's now the moment to know everything. We don't have much time. It's almost over; I can feel it," a voice says from the orb of light, sounding like Abigail.

Abby replies back, "Where are we going?"

"To the past, the beginning—our beginning. You know that, right, Abby? Questions that we both have will be answered."

"Wait...Abigail, our beginning?" Abby says, stunned.

"Abby, what does a friend mean to you?" Abigail sincerely asks.

Abby replys, "A friend is always there for you emotionally. Someone who picks you up when you are down and keeps all of your secrets."

"Then what is a friend supposed to look like?" She pauses, thinking over Abigail's question without an answer. "When I first met Friend, I asked myself that same question before giving him that name—"

"Wait, I thought I was the one who gave him that name?"

"We both did, Abby. Just watch Friend's timeline and it will show you everything."

Abby watches Friend's timeline. She watches Friend fight with Buru for the first time and lose. She watches how he got his scars and was sentenced to the southern moon, stricken of his name. The time he spent on the moon training, learning his power to battle Buru once more during Purity's revolution. The portal opened by the Eldest Elder to save his life, bringing him to Earth. But his timeline doesn't end there, and all Abby can do is watch.

CHAPTER NINE

Unwanted Home

The portal opens, and Friend runs through. He is surrounded by dense woods with large rocks covered in moss and snow dusted on the tall pine trees. Friend turns to the portal as it shrinks in size, stumbling over himself, but it's too late. The portal closes, and Friend falls on his face, landing in the cold snow. He lets out a huge roar, angry and frustrated the last chance he had to save his planet is now gone, and he doesn't know where he is or why he was placed here.

Friend sighs, his breath turning to vapor in the cold. Snowflakes fall from the tree branches, an environment he has never seen or experienced before. Friend puts out his hand, catching some snowflakes and watching them quickly melt to water. He holds himself tight, trying to keep the warmth of his body in as he looks around for where to go next. Knowing there's no way back home but needing to find a way to get warm, he begins to walk aimlessly. Time passes slowly until he hears cars, foreign to him, whizzing by just beyond the tree line. He walks closer hesitantly.

Snow crunches behind him. It's a deer, but to him, it's a threat. Friend gets ready to fight, but the deer is not interested as it runs away from something else, going past him toward the sound of cars. A short moment of silence occurs as the sound of the deer hopping through the woods dissipates to nothing. Then a loud, piercing screech of tires gripping the road tears through the air, followed by a loud bang, making Friend jump and run toward the sound.

The woods become less dense, opening to a small, isolated two-way road. A car sits in the middle with skid marks on the road from it having spun out. Smoke billows from the car, the front of it destroyed. Car parts and glass litter the street. Further down is the deer, the same deer he just saw in the woods, lying on his side, not moving as blood pools around the head and body.

Friend walks up to the car, not knowing what to expect inside. His hands up, ready to fight, Friend is caught by surprise when he sees a woman on the passenger side, wearing a nice dress and stone necklace, and a man next to her, dressed in a suit with his head resting on the steering wheel. Both are immobile with scratches on their faces from the crash. Eerie howls echo from inside the woods. Friend doesn't have a good feeling about it.

Friend leans forward, resting his hand on top of the woman's head. His palm glows as he sees the story and timeline of her life. There's happiness, joy, and a warm sensation of safety and security, along with laughter. The woman has a young daughter, and the man is also a large part of her life.

Friend returns to the reality of the woman and her cold, dead skin. On the center of the dashboard, he sees a picture. Friend picks it up; it's the man and the woman with the small child from the timeline. He searches inside the car, locking his eyes on the same little girl in the backseat alone. Friend leans closer and confirms she's breathing.

He looks around, but there is no one in sight. Not wanting to leave her behind, he puts his hand on her forehead, fixing her wounds while she is unconscious, and picks up the little girl, cradling her in his arms. She does not make a move or sound. Friend looks farther into the backseat, sees a pink stuffed rabbit, a toy he saw her play with in the timeline, and takes it.

Friend goes back to the woman and grabs the necklace too, as he saw in the family's timeline that the necklace is a big part of her life, and the woman promised the little girl that, one day, she will pass it down to her.

Friend puzzles over where to go next. The howling sounds closer, hungry for their deer. He walks down the road, away from the car, the deer, the shattered glass, with only him and the small girl in his arms. The sirens wail in the background as he walks past a sign saying, “Welcome to Rochester,” before vanishing into thin air.

Friend comes across an old and withered treehouse, falling apart in the middle of the woods, and lays the little girl down inside. He looks at the stuffed animal and the tag located on the bottom of its foot that reads “Abby.” His eyes drift back to the girl, Abby, and he rests the toy on her chest; she instantly curls her arms around it.

Night turns into morning with little Abby opening her eyes, lying on the cold wood floor. Friend hovers over her, grunting and clicking in the back of his throat and tilting his head sideways, curious to know what she is.

“Where’s my mom?” she screams. “Where’s my dad? What did you do to them?!”

Friend jumps into a fighting position as her loud voice makes him feel threatened, not knowing what she’s going to do next.

She starts to cry. “I don’t remember what happened. We were going on vacation, but something ran into the road…and…just a loud bang. Where are my mom and dad?”

Friend picks up the pink stuffed animal and the necklace and hands it to her.

“My mom’s necklace! Where is she?” She stares at Friend expectantly, but he does not speak. Her tears intensify. “Where are my parents? What happened?” Her broken voice rings out with sadness and confusion.

Friend wants to help her but knows he can't do much. He snaps his fingers, bringing her to the scene of her mother and father in the destroyed car with the deer in the street. She runs up to the car, screaming, "Mom! Dad!"

They don't move. Their bodies lean forward limply, and blood plasters the hair on their foreheads. She can see herself in the backseat, also unresponsive. She turns to Friend. "Wake them up! Help!" She reaches her hand to touch her father's suit button, but her hand goes right through him. Abby cries harder. "You need to do something!"

Friend shakes his head no.

Abby stands still in a state of shock, breathing deeply, struggling with the realization her parents are gone. "Were you the one who saved me?"

Friend nods.

"But my parents...who will take care of me? Where will I live?" Abby takes a deep breath, closing her eyes tight as tears roll down her face. Maybe it's all a dream, and she's asleep in the car, her parents alive, and their vacation on the horizon. But when she opens her eyes, the wreck still sits before her, Friend hovering behind her.

Friend groans, putting out his hand for Abby. She spares her parents one last mournful glance before wrapping her arms around Friend's legs, holding him tight. Unused to this feeling of love and warmth, Friend stands awkwardly.

Snapping his fingers, he brings them both back to the treehouse.

"No, no, no!" Abby cries as all she knew fades away.

Friend looks at her distraught face, understanding wanting to go back to change something for the better after being left alone. He stands motionless, not knowing how to console her, and Abby cries herself to sleep, leaving them to suffer in their loneliness together.

She wakes up the next day with the rising sun hitting her face through a crack in the wood. Friend sits on the ground, holding himself to keep warm. Abby looks at him, feeling bad. "You need clothes to keep you warm. We need to go to a town," she says with his head tilting, not understanding what she's saying. "A town like this!" she yells, like he's deaf. She takes a stick and carves on the floor a square with a triangle on top, making a home, and another picture of a shirt. "See, that's a house. We need to find this to find clothes like mine but something that will fit you."

He shivers while he nods, grabbing her hand and making them vanish from the treehouse and reappear in a small town with a sign reading, "Welcome to Maplesville." The town is small, and the buildings are old-fashioned with old wood and old people as if they are part of a different time.

She spins around, looking up at Friend. "If people see you, they might get scared. You can't be seen."

He agrees and uses his powers to stop time.

Abby is shocked and amazed by what she sees. "Wow! You can make all these people stop?"

Friend nods, walking ahead into the town with Abby running behind him.

They stop at a store, looking at the front display of old-fashioned televisions. On one of the television screens, three men perform a jazz number. Friend puts his hand on the glass and speeds up one of the televisions to watch them perform. One man plays the trumpet well, the second man sings, snapping his fingers to the rhythm of the beat, and the other man plays the saxophone. He focuses on the front performer while he belts out the lyrics, Friend tapping his foot and snapping his fingers as he mimics the rhythm of the lead singer.

Abby begins to cheer up, laughing at Friend. "You would look nice in a suit. My dad wore a suit every day. He said it was part of his job." She takes a deep breath, thinking back to her parents, trying to hold back her emotions. "Come on, let's try to find a suit for you." She grabs his hand as they both walk down the street into one of the stores displaying suits and ties.

The people in the store are frozen in their spots as they shop. A worker assists another customer, measuring him. Friend moves with awe through the store, amazed at the suits and ties and different colors of blazers, so eager to touch the fabric. Friend chooses a suit and tie, knowing it's too short at the wrists and ankles but not deterring him from wearing it. Abby picks out a top hat and umbrella, saying, "This will help you hide your face. People here don't have a face like yours." He bends over so she can put the top hat on his head, and she hands him the umbrella.

As they are about to leave, she looks up at Friend and says, "I don't know what to call you." She reaches out her hand. "My name is Abby, and I'm seven years old." He grabs her hand and watches with interest as she shakes their hands up and down. "So, should I give you a name? I don't know what to name you." She drops her head as another wave of sadness hits her but quickly searches for a way to distract herself.

Friend puts his hand on her head, and her eyes turn blue, a dull look on her face. Her mouth slowly opens in awe as Friend shows her where he came from and what he was before he came to Earth. When her eyes return to their normal green, she smiles, both shocked and amazed.

"So, you're from far away?" Abby points up at the sky.

Friend looks up as well, nodding.

"Are you trying to go back to where you're from?"

Once again, he nods to her question.

"But…who's going to take care of me?" Abby says with tears building up in her eyes, trying to hold it in.

Friend releases a sobering moan, feeling bad for Abby and what she is going through, so he thinks of an idea to cheer her up. Vanishing and reappearing in a blink, Friend displays the necklace from Abby's mother and the pink rabbit found beside her. She smiles and grabs the stuffed animal first, giving it a huge hug. Then she looks up at her mom's necklace woven between his fingers, the teardrop crystal dangling and sparkling in the sunlight. "That was my mom's favorite necklace. She only wore it for special occasions. She said it was her mom's." Abby reaches out for it, but Friend closes his hand around the necklace, while his hand glows bright, storing his powers in the crystal. When he reopens his hand, the necklace glows blue briefly before fading back to normal. Abby only hesitates with apprehension for a second before excitedly grabbing her mom's necklace and putting it around her neck.

"Thank you for everything. You're a nice—" she says, then grins. "That's it! Friend, that's what I'll name you." She gives him a large hug. Friend felt the love and appreciation and, for the first time, smiles as he hugs her back. "Where do we go now?"

As this timeline ends, everything fades to black. A younger voice of Abby is heard in the darkness.

"We need to work on the plan and I'm not getting any younger. Can you feel it? I know you can feel too, it is still far, but we need to act soon. You need to go home and take back what is yours, but we both know I cannot go with you. It has always been a desire of mine, to find a home that I can call my own. The search is hard but there has to be someone out there who can help." As Friend replies, he growls to younger Abby.

Spring flourishes when the next timeline in Friend's memories opens; flowers and trees are blooming, and the grass is a vibrant green. Friend, disguised with a hat and umbrella, and Abby, now eleven, walk down the street of a new location.

"Are you sure this is a good idea?" Abby asks. "We have been traveling together for so long, and this is how it ends?"

Friend nods as he growls, a little concerned.

"She was the only person I touched that looked promising without getting too involved in her past. She has a lot of secrets as well. She was a part of the secret war," she says about a woman shopping across the street. She leans over, giving Friend a warm, uplifting hug. "I hope this works, but at the same time, I don't want to see you go." She gets emotional, looking up at Friend with her large, green eyes before letting go to encounter the woman.

Abby smooths down her spring, floral clothes. Nervous and trying to blend in with the rest of the crowd window shopping along the main road, she looks across the street at a young lady in a small clothing store, browsing through spring dresses. Crossing the street, Abby builds up her confidence as she rehearses what to say as she walks up beside her. "Hi, my name is Abby. What's yours?"

The lady is caught by surprise, startled by her sudden introduction. "Oh, well, hello. My name is Isabelle but Izzy for short. You need help with anything?"

"Uh, yes, I do. I was wondering, uh…"

"Do you need the police?"

"No, no! You see, I have been traveling for a long time and was just wondering, do you know where there's a place to stay, like a hotel?"

"Where are your parents?"

"It's a long story, and I don't have time to explain. Do you think you can help me out?"

"I can, but I just can't let you go like this. It's strange you came to me out of all people to ask this type of question, and I just can't let you walk around without a parent knowing where you are."

Abby looks disappointed. "I understand. You're not the first one who said that to me. I'll just look for myself then."

"No, wait!" Izzy takes a long pause and continues, "Maybe I can help you. Stay with me for a couple of days until we can situate you somewhere else. What do you say?"

"Wow, really? You would really do that for me?"

"Yes, I wouldn't want you to be out overnight."

"This really means a lot to me. I knew you were a nice person!"

"Oh, yeah? How would you know that?" Izzy asks with a playful smile.

"I bumped into you and saw something different in your timeline—" She clamped her mouth shut, then bit her lip. "I think I said too much."

Izzy tilts her head, trying to comprehend what she is saying. "So, you're a psychic?"

Abby looks around, happy she didn't scare Izzy away. "Yeah, a psychic."

Izzy takes in a deep breath. "Okay. I would like to know, at some point, where your parents are, but for now, you can spend time with me shopping. I can get to know you, and we'll take it from there, okay, Abby?"

"Okay, sounds good to me!" Abby looks over her shoulder at Friend still standing across the street with the umbrella over his head, suddenly disappearing. "Goodbye, Friend," Abby whispers to herself, a sad smile on her lips.

"Are you ready to go?" Izzy says.

"Yeah, I guess I am," Abby replies with a big smile on her face.

Time fast-forwards to Abby sitting in Izzy's dining room, coloring with Izzy, laughing and having a good time. "So your friend is from a planet called Purity, and his planet is under attack by Buru, who stole light from his planet that will kill all life there, and he is waiting for a portal to open to bring him back…ha! Abby, you are too funny. One day, you should write a book of your stories." Izzy laughs.

"Do you have any stories?" Abby asks.

Izzy thinks, then sighs. "Yeah, I do. Years ago, far away from here, I was the youngest in my village to join a war that needed to be fought. I was in a squad of five on a mission that was, and still is, top secret, but all I can say is if it wasn't for me and my squad, life would have been much different. My story is long, just like yours, Abby. When we left the war, I moved to a town. I told my story, and they put up a statue in honor of my sacrifice, but it became too much attention for me. Some didn't believe my fight and my sacrifice, so I left that town and everything I knew behind. We're not that different, you and I, Abby. Maybe that's why we get along so well."

"Yeah, maybe. You're like an older sister I never had." They smile at each other.

Izzy's smile fades slightly. "Abby, how do you know so much about me?" she says, confused.

The front door opens, and Izzy's face turns cold, straight-faced. "Abby, go to the yard, and I'll be there in a second." Sensing something's wrong, she runs out the back door into the junk-filled, grassy yard.

Right when the door closes behind Abby, a man walks into the dining room, a stern, angry look on his face. He looks down at the drawings strewn across the table. "What are those?"

"Please relax. There was a young girl who came to me, and she said she needed help—"

"Help? Everyone needs help, but no one is ever willing to help us. What do you think someone would say if they looked for their kid and found it here? They would think we were kidnapping."

"But I did help her. She's outside. She just needs to stay here a couple of days."

The man's eyes grow large. "Here? She isn't staying here! Hell, no one's staying here. Just me and you. She can go back to her parents where she belongs."

"But that's the thing. I don't think she has parents. I don't know what really happened; she won't say. All she talks about is her friend."

The man reaches into his back pocket, pulls out a pack of cigarettes, picks one out of the almost-empty box, and puts it in his mouth, quick to light it. He takes a second to think with smoke coming from his nose and mouth. "Then where is she?"

"Abby, can you come here?" Izzy calls from inside.

Abby begins to walk in, then stops at the snapping of branches in the woods. "Friend, is that you?" But it's just a squirrel, running out of the tall grass. Abby already misses him and wonders what he's doing now without her.

"Abby!"

"I'm coming!" She runs back into the home, and standing beside Izzy is the tall, stern man.

"Abby, this is Richard."

She waves at him.

The man gives her a disgusted, snarling look, then walks away into the kitchen, and opens the refrigerator. Abby hears the hiss of a bottle opening and a bottle cap hitting the countertop. "So where are your parents?"

"It's a long story," Abby says with her head down.

"Are you from around here?"

"No."

"Where are you from?"

"Richard, I think that's enough," Izzy snaps at him.

"I have one more question. How long are you planning on staying?" Tension flares as an awkward silence sets in with Izzy and Richard both staring at her, waiting for a response.

"Umm, not long," she says.

Richard snarls in disgust as he walks away.

"I'm sorry, Abby. He's not really that polite of a person. Don't take it to heart. Come, I'll show you where the couch is, and you can sleep there for the night and see what tomorrow will bring us."

Abby nods, following Izzy to the living room.

Time jumps to Abby lying on the couch with a pillow and blanket. The yelling from upstairs booms above her. Abby cannot make out the exact words, but Richard seems very angry at Izzy.

Suddenly, footsteps creak down the stairs. Abby throws the covers over her head, leaving a little opening to see who it is as she pretends to sleep. Izzy appears, distraught and sniffling, trying to hold her tears back. She walks out the front door and sits on the front porch. Everything becomes very quiet and still. Abby's barely able to hear the sniffling outside over the sound of raindrops against the windows.

Izzy clears her eyes and looks up to a tall figure standing across the street, looking right at her house. It's Friend, having heard the commotion and ready to protect Abby if need be. "Hey, it's you! The one staring at me when Abby first came to me." Izzy runs through the pouring rain to him, water pouring off the ends of his umbrella. She looks up at his face and realizes all the stories Abby told were true.

"You know Abby, don't you?"

Friend nods.

"What happened to her?"

He holds out his hand, his long fingers curling out as his hand begins to glow. Izzy puts out her hand, hovering over Friend's, hesitating. He snatches her hand tight, and her eyes glow as he shares Abby's past with Izzy, showing her the life Friend had with her.

Izzy pulls back her hand quickly as she comes to. She looks at Friend, sad and in disbelief. "I understand, and you did an amazing job taking care of her. I'll try to keep her as long as I can. There may be a time where I have to let her go, but for now, I will take care of her and protect her."

Friend nods as he whimpers, missing her already, before vanishing in thin air.

Some days and weeks pass with Abby still living in Izzy's home and no more appearances from Friend. There have been a lot of fights between Richard and Izzy about her staying. Richard tells Izzy today would be the last day before he kicks Abby out, saying her imaginary friend can take care of her.

During Abby's stay, Richard has proven to not be a nice guy, not even to Izzy. He drinks too much, says a lot of mean things, and threatens her. Abby knows Izzy is trying hard for her to stay at least another week, but Richard is not changing his mind, saying Abby stayed long enough.

Rain begins to pour and thunder grumbles louder as Izzy and Abby watch cartoons in the living room. Lights shine bright through the front windows as a car pulls into the driveway.

Abby jumps to her feet, worried. "Don't worry. I'll take care of you, I promise," Izzy says as the car engine turns off.

"I'm not supposed to be here," Abby says, her voice wobbling from her fear of Richard.

The front door swings open, and Richard's dark silhouette fills the doorway. A strike of lightning illuminates the bottle of alcohol in his hand and the cigarette on his lips.

"You're supposed to be gone, girl. You don't belong here. We helped you long enough. Now get, girl!"

Izzy tries to defend Abby with her words and her body, pulling Abby behind her. Richard storms over, grabbing Abby by the wrist with the smell of alcohol on his breath. He tries to take her off the couch, but Izzy holds onto Abby. Curses ring out as Richard pulls at Izzy's grip. Screams follow, Izzy kicking at him and tears rolling down Abby's cheeks.

Through the commotion, Abby yells out, "Friend, help me!"

Richard lashes out. "Stop talking about your imaginary friend. He is not real!" He gives one last hard tug, ripping Abby from Izzy's hands.

"Let her go! Let her go!" Izzy screams out at the top of her lungs. "She has done nothing wrong. All she needed was some help. Richard, you get out of my house."

Abby continues to call out for Friend, and Richard glares down at her. "Since you want your imaginary friend so badly, why don't you go back to him?" With the cigarette dangling out of his mouth and the harsh smell of alcohol on his breath, Abby is suffocating in his presence.

A deep groan echoes within the house, catching Richard off guard, and all three of them become very silent. "What is that?" Richard asks, his mood escalating from drunken anger to drunken rage. "Who's outside?!"

Abby's necklace starts to glow. "You are not pure, Richard. He can smell it," Abby says as a smile grows on her face.

Friend groans again toward the back of the house with Richard following the noise, swinging open the back door to the yard.

Izzy forcefully grabs Abby's hand. "Come with me, quick. We don't have much time." She leads them to the kitchen where she reaches on top of the refrigerator and pulls out a folder. Inside is a small business card. "I know your friend is real. I look outside my window every night and see him out there. The first night you came to stay and for some nights after, I walked outside and saw him across the street. Abby, I believe you, and I believe every single thing you told me about you and this friend. I can no longer take care of you, and I can no longer go through the abuse, so here is a true place where you can stay. Give this to your friend. I know of it myself. Abby, like I said before, you and I are not that different,—it's why we get along so well, but you need to go to this place. You have to promise me."

Abby nods, knowing this is their final goodbye and trying to hold back her tears.

"I know this place very well, and they will take care of you. It's a small town I grew up in called Morgantown. I lived there after the war. When I was there, I saved a lot of lives and got rewarded for it, but now, well...we have no time for my story. Here, take this. It's the name and address of the place. It's a little far, but I know you'll make it with your friend. Now go, call for him. Go!"

Abby reaches for the business card, then looks at Izzy, fighting back her tears, not wanting to say goodbye. She wraps her arms around Izzy in a huge hug, whispering, "You don't deserve this."

As quickly as Abby says the words, she runs out of the kitchen and right past Richard. He tries to grab her, but Abby is too quick. She leaps into the middle of the yard, inhales as much air as she can, and bellows out that one name.

"Friend!"

The timeline fades to black but it isn't over.

CHAPTER TEN

Fire and Ash

Abby and Friend reappear deep in the woods. With the pouring rain still falling, they seek shelter in a small cove.

"Never again," Abby asserts, shaking water from her hair. "I will never try to live in another stranger's home. I know we have a deal, and this must happen between us, but I am not going to do that again. We did more wrong than good. We have done this too many times, and every time we try, it doesn't work," she rants.

Friend agrees with her, and she continues, "Before I called you, Izzy gave me a card. It's a foster home in Morgantown. She said they would take people like me. I know you can feel Buru is coming, but I think this is the best thing for the both of us."

Friend whimpers, just thinking of having to leave Abby yet again.

"I know, I know. This is hard for you. This is hard for me too. I don't want to see you go." She gives him a long and strong hug.

More whining comes from him as he wraps his arms around her.

"Well, what are we waiting for? Let's find out where this Morgantown place is." Abby pulls out the map she keeps tucked in her pocket, scanning it to find where they are and where Morgantown is. "If we're here, then…I found it, Morgantown. It's not that far away." She circles where the city is located on the map. "We'll leave when the rain stops. Are you okay with that?"

He looks down at her, heaving a big sigh as he agrees. They sit in the cove together as the memory fades.

The day opens with Abby holding the map up against her face, trying to read the directions on a dark, open road. "Welcome to Morgantown" is written on a sign on the side of the road. "We made it!" Abby says excitedly.

They vanish and reappear in town. She looks around in awe. "This is where Izzy was talking about. It's so nice here, right, Friend?"

Friend nods, upset, knowing this may be the end.

Abby can see his sadness but tries to stay positive. "Come on now, we know why we're doing this. We have to stick to the plan." Friend nods.

They walk down the empty street, eventually coming across the foster home, the same address on the business card, but it's closed with the sign stating they open at 9:00 a.m.

"Well, good news. I guess we're going to have to wait a little longer until the doors open." Friend gets ready to speed up the minutes so the doors can be open, but Abby stops him. "No, let's spend this time together and watch the sunrise."

He smiles, loving the idea, as he wraps his arm around her, and they both turn around, walking down the street.

Soon after, they come across Izzy's statue in Court Square. Abby is in awe over how large her statue is as it salutes the courthouse on the far end of the courtyard. They both stop in front of the statue.

"Do you think we did the right thing? You know, with Richard? He wasn't pure, especially with her." Abby stares at the statue's face, thinking about Izzy. "I didn't tell you this, but I touched Richard's hand when he passed out on the couch one night and looked through his timeline. He was evil at heart, and there was nothing anyone could do to change him."

Friend shakes his head, agreeing with her.

"Yeah, I didn't think so."

An awkward silence looms between them as they both feel this is the last time they will see each other, soon having to say goodbye. "The mission was for me to help you get strong to fight Buru and for you to help take care of me, which you have. Years have gone by, and we helped each other as friends to get through it all. If it wasn't for you coming into my life, I don't know where I would be, and I don't want to know. This mission came to an end so fast, I think, for the both of us. The portal will open soon, and you want to make sure I am safe before you leave Earth."

Abby takes a breath. "I'll ask one more time: can you train me so I can fight with you? I know you're going to say no, but Izzy told me she fought as a soldier for what is right. That's why her statue stands here. She had passion to make sure the people in this town were safe, and I believe she's right that we are not that different. I'm passionate about our friendship; I would do anything to make sure you are okay like how you've done for me, protecting me for so long, and I would like to do the same back. Before you give me an answer, just think about it."

Friend stays unresponsive, deeply thinking about her words. He holds the business card in his hand as the warm summer sun begins to rise.

Ping swoops over their heads and lands in the courtyard. "Friend, look, it's that bird again. Can you feel it, the power that comes from it?"

Friend nods.

"Do you think he knows?"

Friend groans, nodding.

"Yeah, I think you're right. Hopefully, the Elders are on our side."

He agrees as she takes out her journal, opens to the final pages, and begins to write.

While she is distracted, Friend contemplates the business card between his fingers, making up his mind. With a large sigh, he speeds time to 9:00 a.m. when the doors open to the foster home. Friend taps on Abby's shoulder and points at the large clock over Court Square.

"Well, I guess it's time."

He shakes his head.

"What are you trying to tell me? This was the plan. If you don't want me to go, that means we have to work together to fight Buru."

Friend takes a long pause.

Her eyes widen, happy to know he does not want to give her up so fast. "I'll fight with you. I can use your harvested energy in the necklace to help you fight back. Show me how and I will help. That's what friends do. But let's stay here in Morgantown, just in case we change our minds. I am sick and tired of constantly running, so let's stay here. There are plenty of woods to seek shelter in, and we can call it our own. It's something Izzy would want," Abby says while looking up at the statue. "So what do you say, Friend? Let's get ready together."

Friend nods, and they quickly vanish from the courtyard as the scene fades.

Friend's memory goes in and out with different moments of them in the woods as they work together on making a treehouse and the early stages of training. The memory refocuses on Abby, who is now fourteen years of age. She sits in the treehouse as she writes in her journal, her pink stuffed rabbit beside her, dirty and worn through their travels. "Soon, I'm going to need a new journal, Friend. I only have two pages left."

Friend smiles as he leaves the treehouse. She finishes her last sentence in her book and disappears and reappears outside beside Friend.

"Are we training today?"

Friend nods before vanishing and reappearing behind Abby, pushing her to the ground.

"Hey! What was that for?"

She turns, but Friend's not there. Abby smiles, knowing this is a game. Her necklace glows on her command, in control of the power within the necklace as she slows down time to try and find him. Friend reappears behind her, but she is much quicker than he expected. She spins around, sees Friend, then quickly vanishes onto Friend's back.

"I got you this time!"

Friend seems surprised, disappearing with Abby free falling to the ground. Abby gets up, flicking her wrist, and her hands and eyes glow blue, just like Friend's, concentrating, ready to train.

Birds erupt from the branches in a panic, screeching as they fly overhead beyond the tops of the trees. Her eyes and hands stop glowing, and Friend reappears, both of them looking up at the birds. Abby takes a deep breath. "Can you feel it?" Abby says as Friend groans. His memories fade to black.

The scene comes to with Abby sleeping in the corner of the treehouse and Friend sleeping on the opposite side. The treehouse walls begin to glow red as light erupts off her necklace. She wakes up to the glowing, startled. "It's time! Friend, wake up. We need to go. We have to figure out where the portal will open."

Branches break outside of the treehouse, followed by thumping footsteps. It sounds like a group of people. Or a creature with multiple legs. Abby looks outside and sees a chatter heading in their direction. Friend stands upright, angry and determined, knowing Buru is coming. "He must have come out of a portal. Would it be the same portal Buru comes out of?"

He points at Abby's necklace as it stretches straight out, glowing red toward Morgantown.

"Oh, no, this is not good. There're too many people in the town. We need to go now before Buru gets there."

They both vanish as they try to follow where the necklace is pointing. Abby and Friend appear in the Court Square. People in the courtyard stumble back at the sight of Friend, some screaming, others in shock over seeing them appear out of thin air.

"No, no, no! Not here. So many people can get hurt," Abby says, concerned about everyone's safety and well-being. "You all need to leave now! Seek shelter!" she yells out, trying to warn them of the dangers ahead. Some run while others stand by, frozen. "Go, go!" She tries to chase away the last remaining people, but some just won't move.

A sound crackles from the side of the statue as the portal opens. Her necklace glows red as they stand side-by-side with their powers charged and ready. Swirls of purple fill the portal as it opens larger. Deep laughter rumbles from within.

"So, we meet again, brother."

"Show yourself!" Abby yells.

Friend roars in rage and runs full speed toward the portal, catching Abby off guard as his emotions get the better of him. Suddenly, he gets pushed back with a mighty blow to his chest, tossing him twice the length he ran, but he is quick to get up, roaring louder as his eye sockets and mouth glow brighter.

Buru appears through the portal, wearing his armor from head to toe. He takes in a deep breath of air. "I can smell how strong you have become here on this disgusting planet. How long has it been since you met my wrath? It's been so long I can barely remember. You missed a lot, brother, me being ruler of Purity. The people now call me the God of all Gods, Purity still glows red in honor of my power. Only the people who died from the color red are the weak, and there is no need for the weak on our planet. As I look at you standing here beside that small parasite, I know you would never be a good ruler. I see you share your power. Pathetic. Do you think you can take me down with this?" Buru bellows with laughter. "You're too soft with the powers you truly have. I should have finished you off the first time we fought. You are dead in the minds of the people who live on Purity, but I came back to finish you off so I don't ever have to think of you and your pathetic life ever again."

Friend snarls at Buru as he sprints toward him.

"You never learn, do you?" Buru says as he charges, his hands sparking with electricity. As Buru swings his mighty fists, Friend quickly vanishes, inches from being hit, and reappears behind Buru with his leg swinging and smashing on the back of Buru's heavily armored head. Before he can even react, Friend disappears again, Buru looks around frantically. Quick to frustration, Buru aims a shot at Abby, a beam of light hurtling out of his hand. Friend reappears, trying to push down Buru's hand to redirect the beam, but he's too late.

Abby raises her arms in an X-formation, a blue shield of power forming in front of her. The beam hits the shield with so much force her feet slide back, but she holds her ground as the light fades, the shield too strong for it.

Abby searches around and sees a man hiding behind a park bench, too scared to move. "Leave now!" Abby yells out, trying to evacuate the courtyard so no one gets hurt.

Friend continues to attack Buru, who blinks around him, as it is hard to predict Friend's movements.

"That's enough!" Buru roars. A wave of electricity pulses out of his body, knocking Friend back, but he's quick to get back up.

Seeing that Buru remains unscathed because of his armor, Abby vanishes as they continue to fight and reappears on Buru's shoulders, lifting up his heavy helmet.

"Hit him now!" Abby yells out.

Friend materializes before Buru, fist clenched, and sends a full, powerful swing at his face, Buru stumbles back from the force.

Buru groans in pain, smirking. "Is that all you've got? I thought you wanted to kill me," Buru says while splitting his body; there's now three of him. "Come at me, brother."

Friend stands next to Abby to regroup. "You remember our training?" Abby asks confidently.

Friend looks down at her, nodding his head.

"Then what are we waiting for? Let's do this."

She smirks as she inhales heavily, letting out a huge roar alongside Friend, catching Buru by surprise as they run toward him and his duplicates. Abby fights one of the duplicates, winning against him as he disintegrates into a mini explosion of electricity, while Friend takes on Buru and his other duplicate. He is outnumbered and lost, not knowing which one is the real Buru.

As Abby runs to help, the real Buru gets behind Friend, grasping his face and shooting an electrical charge through Friend, who roars in pain. An explosion-like pulse pushes Friend and Buru apart, Friend flying up into the air with no control. Braced in a fighting stance with his feet electrically charged, Buru crouches and springs up into the air. He grabs Friend and flips his lifeless body toward the ground as he yells out, "You cannot kill the God of all Gods. I am the purest. I am Buru!"

He kicks Friend's body back to the ground, and he begins to charge his powers, glowing red with the unthinkable. Buru saturates his body to the point of explosion, waves of energy coming off him.

Abby quickly slows down time as the pulse of energy comes over her and Friend's lifeless body hits the ground. Her eyes glow, and she raises her glowing hands, making a force field dome over the courtyard just in time. The blast spreads over Abby's dome harmlessly but completely decimates everything around it.

"No!" Abby yells, and she watches everything outside of the dome turn to fire and ash. Portals open with Buru's army flooding out of them.

Friend begins to move, struggling to get up. Abby runs over to him. "Friend! Don't move. I'll help you. I don't have much power left, but here, heal up." Abby shields him with his own dome around him, helping him to heal.

Buru cackles. "Foolish parasite, giving a stricken a name and purpose when he was banished from Purity. He is not pure—"

"Yes, he is! He is more than pure. He's a friend; someone you can call on to always have your back; someone who is kind and loving and would never want anything bad to happen to you or your relationship. That is what a friend is, and that's who he is, and that's his name," she snaps back at the ruthless tyrant, making sure he does not get the last word. "You are too small to know the truth."

He says, snarling at Abby, "You're lying!"

Abby screams at Buru and runs full speed toward him as her anger gets the best of her. Buru charges his powers as they run head-on. Buru lifts up his arm, shooting a blast at her, but she dodges, vanishing and reappearing, kicking his arm down and forcing Buru's next shot into the ground. The impact sends him flying into the air. As Abby looks up at him, he takes another shot at her but misses, shooting the statue of Izzy, rubble glittering the sky.

She slows down time as she jumps across pieces of debris and works her way up to him. Reappearing before him and placing her hands on his face, she yells, "Enough is enough," her own blue beam of light shooting out of her hands. She vanishes again. Buru hits the ground hard as his body skips along the courtyard. She reappears on the ground, uninjured as she pants, exhausted from fighting.

He stays down on the ground as he begins to laugh. "You think you know everything, don't you? What we've gone through, me and my stricken brother. You don't know anything."

"I do. He showed me every—"

"He showed you what he wanted to show you. Do you not see? Do you not understand his power? He can manipulate time. He can show you what he wants to sell his innocence when he is at fault. Every day, we were sworn to protect something fake, something that was never there, not knowing how many years had passed from the truth. I wanted change, we all wanted change, but he wanted to stay stuck in a fake life with fake honor. Why believe something that is not there? That's what the purest would say before I took over, before I became God of all Gods, before I made it whole, fighting wars against those who threaten us. That's what we've become, and that's what we've been wanting, to show our power, something he would never show you. He is evil, just like me. He would kill with no hesitation. He's a murderer, a sociopathic serial killer with such strong power gone to waste as he tries to live like he doesn't know who we really are."

"You're wrong. That's not the Friend I know."

"You know he's the one in control of his power and showing you what life he lived, splitting it up into fragments, all leading up to one common goal, a belief that he's the purest of all pure. Fighting so hard to become the new leader, the new God, knowing I would be the one to fight him for it. Why do you think he's trying so hard to come back? Stricken from the southern moon seeking justice? No, parasite, that's not his goal. He wants to be the purest, to lift up his name from a stricken to a god higher than all Nobles, and you're just the one helping him get to that goal." Buru struggles to get up, badly injured as his words make Abby think deeply about who Friend is.

"You're lying," she says, clenching her teeth and charging the energy from her jewelry. Her necklace flickers weakly. She is out of power after healing Friend and protecting Court Square. "No," Abby hisses in frustration. Feeling a tap on her back, she looks up, and Friend stands tall, fully recovered, giving her a reassuring nod that he's there for her, his eyes and hands aglow with power.

Friend roars, vanishing and reappearing behind Buru. His power knocks Buru in every which direction, too slow to keep up. They smash each other into the ground, shooting their colored beams of power, dealing grueling, bone-crushing blows, but with every hit Buru lands, Friend is quick to restore his wounds and broken bones. Friend is now winning the battle he's been waiting for.

Friend pins Buru down to the ground as he gasps for air, beaten bloody as Friend continuously punches his face. Buru turns his head to Abby, his hand moving in her direction as he charges his power for a last-ditch effort.

"Friend!" Abby cries out.

Friend follows Abby's finger pointing at Buru's hand.

"You are still weak, brother," Buru says.

A beam of red electricity pulses out of his hand, heading right toward Abby. She lifts her hands to defend herself, but her necklace is out of power. Friend quickly vanishes, trying to take the shot for her, but the light grazes Friend's side and heads right toward her as he falls. The beam of light hits her in the chest, cracking her necklace as she hits the ground, not moving. Friend clutches his side, looking over at Abby and her lifeless body as he struggles to get to her.

Buru begins to laugh to himself. "You're too soft to be ruler." He gasps for air through his injuries.

Friend hastily gets up from the ground as he limps his way to her, holding his side. He reaches her unresponsive body, and he tries to shake her to wake her up, but nothing happens. He collapses to his knees, letting out a heart-wrenching roar as Abby takes her final breath. His powers are too weak to bring her back and heal her wounds, and Friend knows he cannot go back in time because it will change the outcome of events in defeating Buru.

"You know what you have to do, brother. Choose defeating me or saving your precious parasite. You can't have it both ways. What do you think will happen if Purity finds me dead with no ruler? It would be complete chaos with no ruler, so what is it going to be? Purity—your home planet—or this planet?"

CHAPTER ELEVEN

A True Friend

Friend stays very still, collapsing to his knees as he cradles her lifeless body to his chest and weeps. He caresses her face, feeling her warm skin grow cold. He takes in a deep breath as he looks up at the portal, then back down to Abby. He makes his decision. Friend takes off her cracked necklace, holding it close to him as it starts glowing blue and removing the last bit of energy left in it.

"I see you made up your mind," Buru says, but Friend ignores him as he puts his hand on Abby's face, brushing the hair away from her eyes.

He places his hand on her forehead as he weeps. Abby's body begins to glow bright as her skin cracks and her body falls apart into ash. Friend absorbs the energy within Abby as the wind catches the ash of her body, and she drifts into nonexistence. He collects all of the memories they have had together as her time is now over, storing them inside himself as he is too weak and unable to store them into her cracked necklace. His body glows blue with all the power within him, and he begins to pant under the weight of the reality that his friend is gone. He appears in front of Buru, roaring with rage and grief.

"Do it, brother. This is what you've always wanted," Buru says, knowing his life is also coming to an end. Friend lifts Buru by his chest plate and, with Abby's necklace woven between his fingers, beats him in the face over and over again.

"Stricken, it's you," Friend hears behind him, coming from the portal. Friend turns to the Eldest Elder, looking from the other side of the portal, staring right at Friend. "I have been watching you this whole time. It was me, the bird." Friend releases Buru's unconscious body and walks over to the Eldest waiting for him at the portal. "We were trying to find you for so long, and we were losing hope until one of the Elders felt your power, and that brought us here. I'm sorry for what has happened. It's all my fault. I am the one who brought you here." The realization that the portal that transported Friend to Earth belonged to his supposed ally hits him like Buru's electricity, and he roars in his anger, flustering the Eldest. "But you were outnumbered. I was the one who saw Buru's cheap fight. You would have died."

Friend remains unmoved.

The Eldest sighs. "Listen, I know you are angry, and I can understand that…I saw everything; I saw her die; I saw how she means more to you than anything else. I can't believe I'm going to say this, but I know you're torn between saving Purity and saving this planet. I will take care of Buru, and you take care of her. I will come back for you, I promise, and take you back, but it's going to take time."

Friend calms down as he thinks of Abby's second chance. He looks down at her cracked necklace, thinking long and hard.

"We don't have much time. What do you say?"

Friend nods as he vanishes and reappears next to Buru, grabbing his armor plate, dragging him across the ground like a limp doll, and throwing him into the portal.

"I promise I'll take care of him and come back for you. He will be stricken to the southern moon where he will be left for dead and never seen again."

The Eldest looks down at Buru's body, but he is not on the other side of the portal. "Where did he go? Stricken, he vanished to run away like a coward; another one of his tricks. He might still be on Earth."

Friend looks around the courtyard but is drawn back to the portal at the Eldest's shocked scream. He turns in time to see a bolt of red lightning arc through the air in the portal.

"He's here, on Purity. His army let him escape. Elders, we must capture Buru while he is injured," the Eldest says, motioning at the portal, and it begins to close. Friend reaches out to jump through, to go back to Purity, still feeling like they are in danger, but it closes as the Eldest yells out, "I'll come back for you!"

Friend collapses through empty air as the portal disappears, his wound a striking pain in his side. He looks around the fire and ash town of Morgantown, contemplating what to do next and where to go.

"You did this." A man crawls out from behind a bench, one of the few people who stayed within the dome and survived the blast. "You've killed all that we've known. My wife and my kids are gone, all gone because of you."

Friend ignores the man as he struggles to lift himself up. He looks down at the cracked necklace, closes his hand tight, and snaps his fingers as time moves in reverse. The statue pieces fly back into place, reforming the statue, and Morgantown slowly comes back to life.

"What about me? My kids, Molly, Jacob, Sarah..." the man whimpers as everything goes white, and Friend goes back in time to when he met Abby for the very first time.

He reappears in the woods where it all started. The sudden shock of pain in his side reminds him of the wound there. He is running out of power and needs to conserve it to finish his mission to bring back what is right, something he should have done since the very beginning.

Wheels screech on the road not too far away from him. He reaches the car where young seven-year-old Abby lies unconscious in the backseat. He takes the necklace from the mother, not cracked or damaged, and picks up young Abby and the pink stuffed rabbit, holding her close and tight. Reaching into his blazer pocket, he pulls out the business card Izzy gave Abby. Friend groans and whimpers as he looks deep into young Abby's face, remembering all the times they had and how they're all gone, and on top of that, he failed his mission to ensure her safety, regretting not bringing her to Morgantown's foster care facility.

The ambulance wails in the distance, and the howls of the wolves sound nearby. Friend vanishes to bring Abby to Morgantown.

He reappears, gravely wounded and his powers running out. He faces the foster care building and looks down at Abby as she slowly begins to wake. Abby's voice in his head replays the last time they were here together, "Let's stay here…we can call it our own." His hearts aches, knowing this time it's going to be different.

Little Abby opens her eyes, looking up at Friend but too weak to react. Friend knows she won't remember who he is, and it's for the best. Instead, she deserves to start a new life without him. He places her on the front steps and wraps the new, uncracked necklace around her neck. Curling his fingers around the crystal, he stores his remaining power into it, feeling less whole, like losing Abby all over again. His hand absentmindedly presses over his heart, but he tries to find reassurance that he'll be able to follow his power to know where she is. He places the stuffed rabbit in her hand; she stands there in a daze, the rabbit dangling and dragging against the steps. With one last hug goodbye, he knocks on the front door three times, and he stays with her just a little longer before footsteps approach the door.

A woman answers, who looks down and sees Abby standing there alone with the necklace around her neck and the pink stuffed rabbit in her hand. "Hello there, what's your name?"

"Abby."

"Well, Abby, where are your parents?"

"I don't know. I can't remember?" Young Abby begins to cry.

As the memory fades, it goes to the woods where Friend collapses to the ground in pain, feeling weak. The injury on his side grows more intense, and the only way he can think of helping it is by risking going farther into the future, closer to the time the portal will be open, and regaining his strength from the power in time. Friend uses a tree to help himself up off the ground and stretches out his arms with his hands glowing. Using what little drops of power remain in his body, he forms a sphere around himself and curls up inside to hibernate and heal until the time comes for the portal to open.

The seasons change, and the sun rotates through the sky rapidly from day to night, hundreds upon hundreds of times until it slows down to Friend waking up from his slumber. The sphere around him disappears as he stands on his feet for the first time in many years, the pain of his wound stabbing him, still open and still healing. He tries out his powers. His hands glow for a second before flickering out; his powers are still low, not regenerating as fast as they would on his home planet. Friend knows he cannot last like this. Even if the portal opens, he would not be able to fight. He has his powers in Abby's necklace. He doesn't want to bother her new life but is curious to find out how she is doing. He whimpers just thinking about Abby.

Friend perks up as he senses power coming from the Eldest, looking through Earth's galaxy for him, but he can feel they are still far. Frustrated as he is left with shooting pain and powerlessness, Friend only has one option: find Abby, get his power back, and regain enough health to fight. Friend lowers his brow as he tries to find where she is. A quick gust of wind breaks through the trees, and he can feel the power coming from the necklace. It's close. Friend takes a deep breath as he tries to focus, putting his body back into the orb to recycle his power, creating a bright blue light. He travels fast in the orb like a comet through the woods, creating shock waves as he breaks the sound barrier. Like rolling thunder, he follows the power through the necklace.

The real Abby returns to the dark room of Friend's memories, in shock over what she saw. Abby thinks aloud, "I died, and he chose me over his own planet."

Abigail's voice replies, "Yes, he did, and he wasn't supposed to."

She turns around and sees herself as the blue orb again. "So you're me, but…Abigail, why didn't you say anything?"

"Yes, I am you. We are each other but from different timelines. I lied to keep us safe. Friend needs this. He needs to go home. He wasn't supposed to show you your life, our life, his life. He was supposed to enter the portal by himself with no help. That was the plan, but he didn't stick with it. Typical."

"When I went to the lighthouse and met you, was that real, and did you know you were going to…?"

"That was really me, and it confirmed my fate. I said my name was Abigail, so we don't share the same name. There can't be two of us if we are the same. I am you, and you are me, but we look different and act different, and that's just because our times and lives are different. I knew I was going to die, but I was still focused on training so Friend could go home, whatever it took. I didn't know he would put me into the necklace and for it to work. I still don't want him to know. I don't want him to change his mind."

"So, what happens next?"

"Well, he's going to go through the portal and most likely never come back. He has to fight his brother to save his dying planet."

"What about me? What do I do next?"

"Live your life and move forward. I know he's your friend, and he's my friend too, but he has to go home. Lives are at stake here and on his home planet. I will be with you, and I can show you everything I learned from him. We can be friends too." Abby agrees as the darkness turns white around her, and she comes back to Court Square.

Abby's eyes dim from bright blue to green as she transitions back to her reality, standing on the courthouse steps. Some officers are wounded while others still have their guns drawn, paused in time. Her eyes dilate when she comes across a revelation in her discovery.

"I finally understand, but why would you hide something like this from me?" Abby questions, looking up at Friend.

He growls and clicks as Abigail translates, "He says, 'It's because my destiny is to go home, but reliving this moment has reminded me you deserve to live a normal life. The thought of leaving without you, unaware of your past, would bury me in guilt.'"

"So this entire time you knew I wouldn't remember?"

He nods, pointing at her necklace, frowning.

Abigail translates once more, "He knew your relationship would not be as it once was, but he attempted to restore some of the memories and adventures in your necklace. Aware of the risk involved, Friend attempted to bring you back. Well…bring me back from the dead. In doing so, he sacrificed the safety of his home planet. Although his departure will be coming soon, he didn't want to leave Earth without this unresolved mission. Friend has to resume time in order for the portal to open." Abigail's voice sounds like it is made of gravel, her clear tone undercut with a choking heaviness that forces her to pause several times as she's translating. Abby, overwhelmed with emotion, does not know how to react, as she has kept her promise to not tell Friend about Abigail.

To protect Abby, Friend snaps his fingers, and a gust of wind consumes her as she is no longer on top of the courthouse steps but instead behind the officers. Before she can react, Friend waves his hand upward in a graceful manner, creating a transparent shield protecting himself, before he snaps his fingers, resuming time for the portal to open and ready to protect himself from the officers.

Abby, aware of her powerful potential, feels useless. To prevent any more violence, she thinks of an alternative plan to get the officers' attention. While looking around, she notices how frightened but determined the police officers are as they try to protect their town and each other the best way they know how. Policemen begin reloading their magazines with more ammo as others wait for the command to refire. Some of the officers grab their partners, severely injured with puddles of blood staining the brick ground.

Abby runs to the officer in charge, holding the walkie-talkie to the intercom on his patrol car. "I need your walkie-talkie," Abby demands the officer.

The officer looks up at Abby, speechless and appalled. "How did you escape from the monster?" Other officers' attention draw toward Abby.

"I did not escape, and he is not a monster. He is my friend. I need you to stop firing at him. He needs to save his power for a much greater threat." The officer, not convinced of Friend's intentions, reluctantly hands over the walkie-talkie to Abby.

Abby scrambles for the walkie-talkie. "Wait, cease fire! I know you all think he's dangerous, but he's more than that. He is trying to go home. That noise you hear is a portal, a portal to bring him home."

"Why should we believe you? Look what he did to my men!" one officer responds as he holds a tourniquet around another officer's leg.

Abby responds through the intercom, "I promise he will help you all before he leaves…right, Friend?" Abby asks. He nods to her inquiry and she continues, "He has the power of time, and he has been living here for quite a while now. This is not the first time he has waited for the portal. His last attempt failed, and Earth as we knew it was decimated. He had to choose his home planet or Earth, and he chose us. This is his second attempt, and this time—" She pauses, locking eyes with Friend. "This time, he's going through the portal; that's a promise."

Friend takes in a heavy sigh; supernatural purple sparks appear beside the statue of Izzy. Friend puts his hands up, surrendering his protective shield, as he walks down the steep courthouse steps. The portal slowly opens, catching some officers by surprise, bewildered and disbelieving. Abby drops the walkie-talkie and runs toward Friend.

Friend and Abby meet in the middle beside the portal as it slowly begins to open larger. She looks up at his face, admiring his scars, seeing how much he has sacrificed for her and what belief is on his home planet Purity. Friend deeply focuses on the portal, then to Abby. He kneels to her height and begins to weep, trying to hold it back, knowing it's the end of their adventures. Abby is at a loss for words as she reaches over, embracing his emotions with a warm hug. "You are the best friend anyone could ever ask for. Thank you for your sacrifice."

Friend hugs tighter, feeling Abby's tears pressed onto his scarred face.

Friend lets go, looking at her as he nods, knowing it's time to go before anything comes through the now-opened portal. He reaches into his blazer, pulling out the journal, handing it to Abby. She waves goodbye to him, and Friend waves back as he snaps his fingers, making everything around her go back in time. Friend turns to the portal as he thinks to himself that it's quite surprising Buru didn't emerge from the other side but doesn't deter him. He runs as fast as he can into the portal, jumping through to the other side, and the portal closes behind him. Abby stands still, now feeling more alone than ever as she watches time rewind around her.

As everything around her turns white, Abigail says, "He will be missed. My best friend." Abby looks at the journal and rubs her finger over the added name, "ABIGAIL."

"Time is tricky, Abby, and so is this power," Abigail says. "Since the mission is complete, I can show you even more, but it will take time. I'll be with you through it all as a new friend."

Time reverts back to the morning. Abby relives her last day of school where she meets with her new potential parents, Cole and Julie.

"Abby, they're here. Come on down, girl!" Cece yells from the main floor.

Abby opens her bedroom door. "I'm coming!" she replies in exhilaration. Before Abby can turn around, she hears the sounds of light conversation from both a male and a female's voice approaching her home through her open window. Abby rushes back to her bed and stuffs her bags with the last of her belongings. She struggles to zip up her luggage. Tackling her suitcase shut, she sits on it to finish closing the zipper.

"Abby, do you think it was a little peculiar that nothing was shown on the other side of the portal when it opened?"

"I think he will be fine, Abigail. The Elders must have opened the portal where Buru wouldn't see. He finished the first half of his mission. In the end, that's what we both wanted."

Abby places her overstuffed bag onto the floor, creating a loud thud. She drags her suitcase to her door. Abby takes a minute to look at her now-empty room. She embraces this bittersweet moment, as this will be the last time she will live here. Abby reaches into her back pocket, retrieving a letter she has written for

Cece. She rests the folded letter on her nightstand; on the front, it reads, "Thank you."

She finally makes her way out of her bedroom and starts walking down the stairs. Her palms are sweating, followed by a tingling sensation in her fingers. The closer she gets to the bottom of the steps, the more Abby feels her heart pumping through her chest.

The small talk and laughter become mute when Abby enters the living room. Ms. Perez stands up with a large smile on her face. "Hello, Abby, are you ready?" Abby nods.

Cole and Julie spring up off of the couch. Julie quickly adjusts her dress as Cole stands beside her, awaiting further instruction from Ms. Perez. Cece stands off to the side with the foster care coordinator, the same coordinator who first brought Abby to Cece when she was seven years old.

Julie steps forward to Abby. "Hi, Abby. My name is Julie, and this is Cole, my husband. We are so happy to finally meet you. Ms. Perez tells me you won in the potato sack race at school!"

Abby nods, shy but excited.

The foster coordinator steps forward. "Well, Abby, I hope this time will be the last. Cole and Julie are amazing people and will give you a loving home."

"I promise we don't bite," Cole says, trying to break the tension in the room.

Julie glances at him, trying to discreetly shove his shoulder. "Cut it out."

Abby giggles, finding humor in their interaction.

Cece looks at the time. "Well, it's starting to get late; you have a plane to catch."

Abby notices Cece won't make any eye contact and appears upset. Aware of how difficult this may be for Cece since losing her daughter Amelia, Abby doesn't hesitate, walking over to Cece and giving her a warm hug, catching Cece by surprise. "I want to thank you for opening up your home to me every time

I needed it. I promise you, this time, it will be the last. A promise is a promise."

Cece's tense body melts into Abby's arms, embracing the love. She knows deep down this is the last time they will spend together. "You're very welcome. Now you must go and catch that plane. The last thing I need is for you to miss your flight," Cece says with a shaky tone, as if she were going to cry, and continues, "I don't want to get a knock on my door and see you on the other side."

"Thank you for taking care of her, Ms. Carter. We will make you proud. We will keep you posted with photos and all!"

Abby is eager to start her new adventures, ending this chapter of her life and starting anew. She says her final goodbyes. The coordinator and Ms. Perez help Abby and her new adoptive parents to the door. They all walk out to the taxi that awaits them outside. Abby follows Julie, climbing into the taxi, as Cole attempts to lift her heavy luggage. Abby and Julie laugh as they watch him finally pack all the luggage in the trunk.

Cole hops into the taxi, panting and out of breath. "What did you pack, rocks?" he says, making Abby laugh some more.

"Is everyone ready?" the driver says, taking the car out of park.

"I think we are. What do you say, Abby, you ready?" Julie asks.

"Yeah, I think I am," Abby replies with a smile.

The taxi begins to drive away. Abby turns once more, looking out of the back window, where she can see Cece standing on the steps to the brownstone, dabbing her eyes with a tissue, and Abby waves goodbye, a humble moment she will never forget.

Three Years Later

Abby is now seventeen years old, still wearing her crystal necklace around her neck. She lives in Melville with her adoptive parents, Julie and Cole. In the fall, she will start her senior year at Melville High. Her perspective on life has changed. Abby is no longer that quiet, shy person anymore. Instead, she is well-liked and more social than she once was.

The summer sun brings a muggy humidity that makes it unbearable to tolerate the mosquitoes and houseflies in the busy community grocery store. Abby wears a black polo, khaki pants, and a green smock that reads, "Melville Food Market," where she works for the summer. She starts ringing in the items on the conveyor belt and notices there are drinks, ice, burgers, hot dogs, steak, charcoal, plates, napkins, etc., assuming it will be for a backyard barbecue party.

"Abby…is that you?" the gentleman asks while noticing her name tag on the apron.

As Abby looks up, she quickly realizes it's her school principal, Mr. King. "Good morning, Mr. King, how are you?"

"I'm doing well, how about yourself?"

"I'm well," Abby says as she helps bag some of the items.

"So this is your summer gig?"

"Yeah, it is." Abby smiles, taking a sip of her bottled water near the register.

"Have you thought about colleges yet?"

"No, not yet. I still have some time," Abby says while placing some bags into his cart.

"Not the answer I anticipated. The time will be here before you know it."

"I know, but I still have not pinpointed what colleges to enroll to."

"You are multi-talented, Abby. Your good grades, your active participating role as student president, and your commitment to volunteer for our community aid organization are more of a reason to apply sooner. I don't foresee any circumstance where a college would think twice about your admission."

"I'll be sure to look into it, Mr. King. Your total is $85.77," Abby says with a smirk.

"Sure thing." Mr. King hands his credit card over for Abby to process the transaction.

"Stay dry. I heard there is a storm coming."

"I'll try. Thanks for the heads-up. Well then, have a great rest of your day now," Mr. King says, smiling back before wheeling his shopping cart out of the store.

Abby feels a tap on her shoulder. She turns to see her coworker, Zac, standing behind her. "Hey, Abby, you can take your break, and I'll take it from here."

Abby looks up and finds herself admiring his hazel eyes. "Hey, Zac, umm, yeah, okay," she says, fumbling for words while smiling, giving him an awkward wave.

She walks away down aisle thirteen. She stops, looking over the small basic tools, glues, bug sprays, and pest control. Further down, she spots the mouse traps she needs. She inspects up and down the aisle to make sure nobody is in sight. Abby reaches for the mouse traps quickly, stuffs some of them inside her apron pocket, and casually walks away.

She treads into the back of the grocery store, leading to the stockroom. There is an endless supply of food and essential items that were recently delivered to restock the shelves. There is a nearby exit through the back door. When Abby leaves the grocery store, she passes the dumpster. The foul odor of expired, unpurchased food reeks next to the loading docks, a place where most don't think to take their break. She sits some distance away from the rank dumpsters on top of some wooden pallets.

"What are we going to do?" Abigail's voice comes to Abby.

"Stop worrying. It's not helping. I am taking it one step at a time. The last thing I want to do is panic and act too fast or irrational."

Their conversation gets interrupted. "Abby, who are you speaking to this time? I think this is the fourth time this week, but who's counting?" It's Anya, another one of Abby's coworkers. Anya is an introvert, typically quiet, but finds an acquaintance in Abby. She looks out for Abby and has gotten closer to her over the summer break. Together, they both achieved the top grades in their class. She sits next to Abby, holding a piece of paper in her hand. "Don't worry, Abby, I'm not going to tell anyone; I just want to know you are okay."

"Wow, those clouds look threatening," Abby responds, trying to gear the conversation to something else. They both look up at the clouds, getting lower and heavier. Hopping off the pallets, they move toward the grocery store to avoid getting caught in the oncoming storm.

"Tell me what's going on."

"Nothing, you know, just a lot on my mind lately."

"You sure? You've been concerning me recently. You know you can talk to me any time."

"Sure, I know. I'm just tired, that's all."

"Okay, well, I might have some news that will cheer you up. I actually came here to ask if you wanted to come to a party I'm throwing next week? There's going to be games, food, and boys!"

I don't know. I'll have to think about it. Are your parents allowing this?"

"Yes, they are. Enough about me, are you coming? Because from the looks of it, you and Zac are getting a little close," Anya says, raising her eyebrows with a grin on her face.

Abby feels a heavy twist in her stomach as her eyes widen and her mouth drops to Anya's blunt speculations. Her cheeks begin to turn red, as she has just been exposed. "Anya, you're crazy! I've no idea what you are talking about. I can't get out a single sentence when he talks to me. I bet he thinks I'm weird or something."

"That's not a no! Just think about it. Every time his shift starts or he gets off his break, he always asks you how you are doing. It has been happening all summer…"

"Wait! You see it too…" Abby, in denial, finally accepts that Anya is right. She blushes. "I knew it!"

Anya's mouth drops. "I mean, he's making it pretty obvious if you ask me. It seems like you are leading him on when you play hard to get."

"I am not," Abby responds with a smile.

"Do you think he knows? I mean, I won't say anything, but if you want me to, I—"

"No, don't even think about it, Anya. You didn't hear anything."

Anya gives Abby a large smile, handing her the invitation. "You have to attend. I can envision it now, the cutest senior couple," she says, teasing Abby, all in good fun.

Abby takes the invitation while glancing at the address and time written in marker. It's obvious this party was a last-minute thought. "There's no funny business about this party, is there, Anya?" Abby asks, slightly apprehensive.

Anya's face shifts from a smile to a frown. "Funny business? No, not at all. Everything will be fine."

"Okay, I'll think about it."

"Don't worry, Abby. This is the perfect opportunity to have fun, and besides, Zac would be pleased." Abby rolls her eyes. "Listen, I got to start restocking the shelves. I'll see you inside." Anya walks back in the store.

Abby looks up and realizes it's now darker than it was a few seconds ago. She pauses in deep thought.

"So what now! "Abigail says, breaking Abby's concentration.

"Not now. My break is over," Abby responds, flustered, trying to be conscious of her tone.

Abigail snaps at Abby, "You can't live both lives! There will be a time when all of this will slip, and you're going to have to choose."

Abby tunes out Abigail's voice and walks back into work to finish the rest of her shift.

Later that afternoon, Abby gathers her belongings from her locker and walks out of the grocery store wearing her red and white polka-dotted rain jacket. She walks over to her bike, sturdy and blue with thick, white-walled tires and a basket and light on the front.

"Hey, do you need a ride home?" a voice says behind her. Turning around, she sees Zac walking to his car. An awkward pause follows as Abby figures out what to say. Zac breaks the silence, looking up at the sky. "The weather is changing, and from the looks of it, I don't think you want to get caught in the rain."

"I think I'll make it. Thank you for the offer," Abby responds, slowing down her words so it is easier for her to speak.

"Okay, then I guess I'll see you tomorrow." Taken aback, Zac walks toward the driver's side.

"See you tomorrow," Abby says while unlocking her bike from the loop wave bike rack. Zac waves at her while driving away. Abby waves back, feeling like she just let herself down, replaying what she should've said.

Shortly after Zac leaves the parking lot, a rumble of thunder is heard in the distance. She hastily hops onto her bike. Droplets of rain begin to fall as the sky darkens, followed by rumbles and flashes of lightning illuminating the road while she rides her bike through town as fast as she can.

Passing through the downtown area, lined with stores, she finally reaches an old train bridge, a landmark to herself that she's halfway home. The navy blue structure is being taken over by mother nature, vines draped over the metal beams, the tracks are corroded, and holes dot the length of the bridge. The train hasn't been used in decades, as it was in place for coal miners who first settled in Melville.

As she approaches her halfway point, the storm opens above her and the clouds dump buckets of torrential rain on top of her. She stops under the old structure, providing her some protection, but the wind picks up, making the rain blow sideways and leaving her vulnerable. She takes a second to catch her breath, tying the strings on her hood tighter, then snaps her fingers just how Friend would, stopping time. The rain droplets freeze in midair like glistening icicles.

Abby rides her bike through the droplets, weaving along a dry path as she makes her way down a residential block where she spots her home, a light-gray house with vinyl siding, dark gray shutters, and white trim around the windows. She rides up the long driveway and parks by the white picket fence. Before entering her home, she snaps her fingers again, resuming time.

When Abby enters, she smells dinner coming from the kitchen. She hangs her jacket and backpack and places her sneakers by the shoe rack.

Julie's voice calls out, "Who's home?"

"It's just me, Julie," Abby says.

Emerging from the kitchen with her curly hair tied up, wearing an apron and oven mitts and sweating, Julie smiles at Abby. "You're pretty dry. You came home just in time. It's just starting to come down now. I am so happy for this storm because this summer heat is a killer. Hopefully, it breaks. So how was your day?"

"It was the same as any other day. I saw Mr. King. He was talking to me about where I was looking to go to college, but I don't know yet."

"Well, you just need some time to figure out what career you may be interested in. We could look up some colleges and make some appointments to see which is the best fit. We still have a little time; don't worry, it will all work out." Abby agrees.

Suddenly, they smell something burning, catching Julie by surprise. "That reminds me, I'm cooking your favorite. Hopefully, it doesn't burn. Just my luck," she says, running back into the kitchen frantically.

Abby laughs aloud as she watches Julie franticly flailing her arms. "Is everything okay?"

"Yeah, the sides are just a little burned. Honey, why don't you wash up for dinner?"

"Okay, Julie, I'll be upstairs." She runs up to her room and locks it behind her. When she looks around, her room is over-the-top organized. Her bed is made, and her wall is covered with awards from school and sports. Some read "First Place" while others read "Best in Class" or "Perfect Attendance." Photo frames sit on her dresser and nightstand of when she, Julie, and Cole went on a little adventure at the town fair. She reminisces on what a great time she had that day.

It was Cole's idea for Abby and Julie to take part in the Melville Winter Fair. They gathered all the materials needed to make the seasonal fair candles. Abby and Julie would wear their aprons as they lined up the soy wax, wicks, wax dye, and essential oils. Every time she glances at the photo, she can remember all the comforting scents they put into the candles. Such as the gingerbread, peppermint, and her favorite scent of them all was cranberry kettle corn. It was their first project together. It was a time in her life where she felt like she finally belonged. All these memories show how far she has come in just a few years.

Before taking off her smock, she reaches into the deep pockets and removes the mouse traps, hiding them in a shoebox under her bed.

"It's been three years now, and there has to be a reason why he's back. Maybe he's in danger?" Abigail says, bombarding her with more questions.

Abby has had enough of Abigail's badgering. "Why don't you ask him yourself since you're so worried?"

"Abby, I'm not trying to attack you in any way, but if he is in danger, that puts you, Cole, and Julie at risk."

"What? I don't want anything to happen to them. They treat me so well, and the last thing I want is for them to know my past. No one would understand." Abby sighs, calming herself down. "You know, there have been times already I've almost called them Mom and Dad. Why is it our lives are most likely in danger?"

"I'm not sure, but I need you to reach out to him sooner rather than later."

Time passes into the evening, and Cole is now home. Julie calls Abby down for dinner. She walks down to the dining room where Cole and Julie sit with their plates of food.

"Hey, kiddo, I already made you a plate," Cole says with his face full of pasta and sauce dripping from his lips.

Abby laughs at Cole and the disgusted look on Julie's face as she smacks her husband's shoulder. "Do you have any manners?"

"What? If you didn't make such good food, I wouldn't be eating like this." They all laugh together. Cole goes for another mouthful, then turns to Abby.

"How was your day at work? Did you get caught in the rain?"

"Not for long. I made it home just in time."

"Anything new happen today?"

"I was invited to a house party by one of my coworkers, Anya. It's supposed to be for the new and upcoming seniors before school starts back up again."

Cole and Julie look at each other with Cole smiling, saying aloud, "Is there a boy involved?"

Abby blushes. "It's just a party. Her parents will be home."

Julie chimes in, backing Cole, "Abby, I've never seen you blush like that. There is definitely a boy involved. What's his name? I bet you it's that one boy...what's his name, Ben...No? Zac, that's it!"

"Stop, it's not like that." They all laugh.

"Okay, Abby, I'll stop teasing you for now. I'm happy you had a good day today."

They go back to eating, and Julie and Cole start talking about work. Abby's mind wanders to her conversation with Abigail. Julie can see Abby is in deep thought as she picks at her food, zoned out.

"Is everything okay?" Julie asks.

Abby hesitates. "There has been something on my mind for quite some time. Is it okay if I call you Mom, and Cole, can I call you Dad?"

Cole and Julie are taken aback "Well, that was random and unexpected," Cole says, looking at Julie, who stares at Abby with watery eyes, nodding yes.

Julie gets up from her chair and walks over to Abby to embrace her with a warm and inviting hug. "You have no idea how long I've wanted you to call me mom," Julie says.

"Come on, Julie, you're going to make me cry," Cole says nervously.

Abby, embracing all the love and warmth they show her, gains reassurance that, no matter what happens, they will love her and accept her, hopefully, even if her secret slips.

Abby gets up from the table, taking her plate with her to the sink. "I'm going to throw out the trash."

"Okay, we'll get some dessert ready," Julie says.

Cole looks out the window, commenting on the weather. "Wow, it's getting really foggy out there. A perfect environment for a monster to hide," he warns, trying to sound spooky and scare her.

"Monsters don't scare me," she says, joking along with him.

Abby ties up the trash and walks to the back door. She softly snaps her fingers, pausing time. She rushes up into her room, grabbing the mouse traps under her bed, then walking back to the kitchen in the same location where she paused time. Snapping her fingers and resuming time, she walks outside into the yard, grabbing the heavy bag of garbage. She follows the pathway to the side of the house where the aluminum trash cans sit next to some bushes. Right above is her bedroom window. As Abby places the trash bag into the garbage bins, she pulls out the mouse traps, loading and placing them under the bushes.

Later that night, the sound of a sudden snap is heard right outside Abby's cracked-open window, waking her from her sleep. She gets up with their hands glowing, stopping time. She flips off her bed sheets, jumps out of bed, grabs a flashlight, and quietly rushes down the stairs.

When Abby approaches the bushes, she finds the large field mouse still trapped there. She gently lifts the metal clamp, releasing the rodent, and holding it by its tail, she runs into the dense fog. She runs as hard and as fast as she can as the air gets even denser, making it hard to navigate and breathe.

She stops abruptly before a towering, skinny, and frail silhouette. She puts out her hand, holding the mouse by its tail. "It's been a long time since I last saw you, and a lot has changed. I know we have a lot more stories to share. Our adventures are just beginning. What do you say, Friend?"

THE END.
WITH NEW ADVENTURES BEGINNING.